Rum, Rome and Rebellion

Rum, Rome and Rebellion

THE CHRONICLE OF A PIOUS PILGRIMAGE

told by *Adalbert Seipolt*
translated by *Anthony Harryman*
illustrated by *Polycarp Uehlein*

SHEED & WARD—NEW YORK

Library of Congress Catalog Card Number 63-8541

Manufactured in the United States of America

To the friends of my student days
in Rome
and to one in particular

Contents

Those travelling include

THE HONOURABLE CLERICS

Monsignor Schwiefele, a dignitary of Swabian coinage. There should be many more like him.

Harald Schlüter, a chaplain of Rhenish Prussian lineage. There are many like him.

Alois Süss, made reverend only a week ago.

THE AMIABLE LADIES

Baroness von Neuhaus, whose heart beats for Rome and Hapsburg.

Alwine Raibeisen, her right hand armed with a red pencil, and her left with her daughter.

Sulamith, distinguished more for her knowledge than her education.

Emerenz Obermair, a maiden advanced in

years, full of enthusiasm for indulgences and a drop of the best.

Eve, a maiden young in years, a medical student, whose character is revealed only in the course of the journey.

THE REMARKABLE LAYMEN

Baron von Neuhaus, with the most important name of Ferdinand, allowed to accompany his wife.

Adam Birnmoser, lay organizer of the trip, and its happy victim.

Luitpold, an upright sacristan from Munich and

Simmerl, a hop-farmer from the Hallertau, two worthy representatives of a worthy breed.

ONE ADMIRABLE SISTER

one alone, for which reason she deserves all our affection:

Sister Annaberta Vogelwieser from the Bavarian forest.

1. *Concerning the pleasures of acquaintance, or why the schoolmistress reached for the communication cord*

"It's worse here than the school playground," Sister Annaberta, whose family name was Vogelwieser, murmured to herself as, clutching the hand of Reverend Mother Potentia, she strove to fight her way through the crowds at the main station in Munich. An elderly, plumpish, and moreover short-sighted child of God, she would hardly have managed on her own to locate the platform where the pilgrims' train to Rome awaited her. Reverend Mother Potentia, however, divided the swirling masses of people as the bow of a warship divides the ocean waves, and towed little Annaberta like a barge behind her.

The turmoil reached boiling-point at platform 11. Priests were fluttering nervously about, their coats flying out behind them, gray-haired married couples were surreptitiously exchanging farewell kisses, while the mouths of Tom, Dick and Harry brought forth every deformation of the German language and anxious mothers heaped advice and exhortations on their daughters. The Reverend Mother pushed aside like ninepins whatever crossed her path, steered purposefully towards the nearest ticket-collector, and asked him where Sister Annaberta could find her seat. In the last carriage, was the answer. The two religious hurried to it, for already the loudspeaker was summoning all passengers to board the pilgrims' train and close the doors.

Reverend Mother refused to be discomposed.

"Annaberta, my dear, keep calm. A pilgrimage is not a trip to the October wine festival. You must embark on it with dignity and inner composure. Look, there is an empty seat. Just sit there for now. I shall be back in a moment. I am merely going to inform the leaders of the party that Sister Annaberta Vogelwieser has arrived on time." And already her wimple had vanished into the throng. Annaberta had not finished putting her small case and her bags on the rack before Reverend Mother appeared at the door again.

"All is well," she said. "The monsignor will shortly be visiting each compartment personally to make sure that all the pilgrims are comfortable. I have recommended you to his especial care. So you will not want for anything. And now, God be with you! It is, of course, a little unusual for a sister of our order to undertake such a long journey on her own, but you have really deserved the honor. Think of us when you visit the holy places. And send us a card from anywhere you especially like. You know how much we are looking forward to hearing from you. And try to find a few sound, reliable travelling companions, so that nothing unfortunate happens to you. You know that the children of this world are cleverer than the children of light. And now God bless you, Sister Annaberta."

The door slammed to. The train began to wheeze into motion. In silence, Sister Annaberta shook the Reverend Mother's hand once more through the open window, not knowing whether to laugh or cry. She finally decided to do both.

Those in charge of the pilgrims' train were quartered in the center coach. The official leader was Monsignor Schwiefele, a sturdy, thickset gentleman with conspicuously large feet and a head that seemed to have been borrowed from Goliath. His eyes glittered like the jewel in a bishop's ring, and his already gray hair stood defiantly up on end, making it difficult to detect in him the obedient son of our Mother Church that he indubitably was. This was already his hundred and twenty-

third trip over the Brenner Pass, and he knew the stretch of track from Munich to Rome as intimately as the psalms in his breviary. What made him invaluable as a pilgrimage leader was his knack of striking the right note for every profession, every income group and every temperament, and thus in the twinkling of an eye establishing with each individual pilgrim just the paternal, fraternal or filial relationship that was needed. Except, of course, with such people as that headstrong town chaplain from the Rhineland, who with his parish youth group of both sexes represented a not-to-be-underrated minority among the flock of pilgrims.

This reverend gentleman, Schlüter by name, told the monsignor he would see to it the trip had a "contemporary atmosphere," that any laxity in word and deed would be avoided, and no concessions made to sentimental, old-maidish piety. Not for nothing, he said, had he studied for two years at the German College, and he knew how dangerous Roman slovenliness could be to German religious education. Ergo, he expected those in charge to do all they could to make the journey young in spirit and broadminded. When at the start of the journey this ultimatum (no doubt confirmed in writing beforehand) was hurled at the upright monsignor's head, he first took a deep breath, calmly polished his spectacles in order to look more closely at this remarkable cleric, then said: "All right," thinking to himself the while: "We'll soon deal with you, you Prussian!"

The third of the trio in charge was Herr Adam Birnmoser. He had in his youth spent a few terms trying his hand at theology, then served long years in the infantry, sometimes favored by fortune, sometimes not; and now

he earned his daily bread by organizing special trains, to Oberstdorf in winter, to Cologne at carnival time, to Spain at Easter, to Rome at Whitsun, to Sylt in the summer and to the October wine festival in September. Which permitted him to smoke six strong cigars a day, and to recite a rosary after every second cigar. For Birnmoser was, for his capabilities, quite oppressively pious, never missed an indulgence if he could help it, joined every fraternity, and moved all the pilgrims to tears in the evenings when he sang Gounod's "Ave Maria" through the train loudspeakers.

These "big three," as a wag baptized them, looked after the whole band of pilgrims—Moms, Dads, intellectuals, light-hearted girls. They watched over them body and soul, carrying with them a stock of medicines and also a portable library of morally unimpeachable light reading. It was they too who worked out the details of the program, and then Birnmoser the layman had often to act as mediator between the two reverend gentlemen. For while the monsignor liked to give the pilgrims a breather between engagements and visits, keeping a little elbow-room in the schedule, the chaplain desired to work everything out to the last minute, which made the monsignor furious and roused him to observe that, after all, he had not been born with a stopwatch in his hand.

The chaplain smiled condescendingly, flashing his beautiful teeth, and inquired whether his reverence would care to pronounce the pilgrimage officially open, the train having found its way out of the maze of tracks at the Ostbahnhof and taken course for Kufstein.

The monsignor was about to retort something, but he swallowed his gall, switched on the microphone, crossed himself and began in his powerful voice:

"Beloved pilgrims! In God's name let us begin this pilgrimage to the Eternal City. May it bring great joy and rich blessings, not only to us, but also to our brethren at home who are unable to travel with us, and who are accompanying our train with their good wishes and their prayers. I am now going to visit every compartment so as to get to know each one of your personally. And if you have any worries, you have only to tell me." The journey was thus officially opened. "Come along with me, my dear Birnmoser," the monsignor invited the manager, taking him amicably by the arm, "it will give the reverend chaplain a chance to say his office in peace."

Their visit began at the tip of the train's tail, as Birnmoser was fond of saying. There, meanwhile, Sister Annaberta had made the acquaintance of the children of this world. She was content to be placed in the last carriage. She could thus stay a split second longer in

Germany, and another split second longer in Italy on the way back. The lady opposite her was not in agreement with such logic; in fact she was furious at having to bring up the rear. It meant, she said, that one was always the last to see all the beauties of the landscape, and it was moreover the most dangerous place to be if the train crashed. As was her wont, Sister Annaberta nodded in approval of these pronouncements, about which it was not worthwhile to argue, whatever her own views might have been. The lady felt her indignation justified, and introduced herself as Frau Raibeisen, a schoolmistress. Her outstanding features were a dark green dress, thick, horn-rimmed spectacles, and a set of china-white teeth which she displayed with every pure vowel. What distinguished her from all the other occupants of the compartment was her impeccable German, free of any local accent, and a perfect pronunciation of all foreign words, which in Annaberta's eyes imparted to her an aura of omniscience.

Next to the schoolmistress sat her daughter, a girl of seventeen, who no doubt was very gifted. No doubt, also, it was only this particular morning that she happened to be looking unspeakably stupid and snobbish. Her name was Sulamith. "What a funny name, probably one of those pagan, Germanic names that are all the fashion, like Karin or Helga," Annaberta thought to herself, mentally running over some of her sisters' abstruse names: Eustochium, Glyceria or Afrasia for instance. They, at least, had patrons in heaven.

An elderly married couple had taken the seats to the left of Sulamith. They signed themselves von Neuhaus,

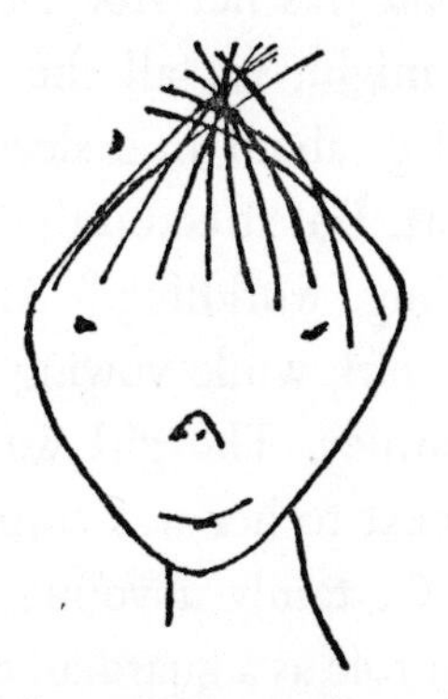

and had the rank of baron and baroness, but had obviously come down in the world. She was half a head taller than he. No wonder he jumped when she scolded him in public: "Ferdinand, your tie is crooked. You can't appear like that in front of the Holy Father." Well, there was still plenty of time. Bulbous steeples and grazing cows were still hurtling past the windows, and as yet no campaniles or loaded donkeys. The sky was not yet a radiant sapphire; on the contrary, it had put on the most modest shades of white and blue at its disposal to wave a sincere farewell to the pilgrims.

The Raibeisens and the impoverished aristocrats made no unpleasant impressions on Annaberta, whereas the girl sitting by the other window aroused her antagonism at first sight. Chestnut hair, scarlet lips, and spinach-green sunglasses—was that supposed to be beautiful? But most offensive of all was her frock. Annaberta was not up in fashion. It might, for all she knew, be the very latest thing to flutter about in a sleeveless, vivid yellow creation of that sort. But it certainly did not conduce to morality. "Worldling, worldling," Annaberta lamented to herself over the girl, while vowing to keep an eye on her during the journey. The girl was as yet unaccompanied. The seat next to her was empty. Who might be going to take it? Certainly a young man. The schoolmistress, too, in her role as a guardian of morality, seemed to be at grips with the same problem. She, a mother thoroughly trained in pedagogy, could not be indifferent to what type of masculine individual sat confined for two days in the same compartment as her daughter.

Yet before their arrival in Rosenheim solved the mystery, the monsignor and Adam Birmoser appeared, greeted each of them in the most friendly way, and asked how they were. The schoolmistress observed through her horn-rimmed glasses that Birnmoser bowed more deeply to the brimstone yellow butterfly at the other window than to her daughter, and she swore to herself that in revenge she would take the very first opportunity to cut him dead. Most ungraciously did she accept the little white card and envelope that the secular member of the organization handed her. "What is this supposed to be?" she asked. Birnmoser began to explain. On the card was printed: "I am travelling to Rome principally in order to . . ." and every pilgrim was then to express in an infinitive clause what he or she thought most important in this journey to Rome, to seal up the envelope carefully, and to hand it back to those in charge. None was to invent a false reason, everyone on the contrary was to speak freely. Only thus could a true picture be obtained of the travellers' real intentions and interests. The sealed envelope was a guarantee of anonymity, and so there need be no fear of ridicule or criticism.

The schoolmistress considered this all wrong, and she declared that ominous indeed was such an application of the questionnaire method to matters of the utmost sanctity. The brimstone yellow at the other window was all the more emphatic in her approbation of thus extending the modern practice of taking Gallup polls to a trainload of pilgrims, and in exchange she received from Birnmoser a thankful (too thankful!) smile. The monsignor added that Birnmoser had already tried out this scheme on a special train to the October wine festival, and very successfully too. With that, the gentlemen in charge of the journey took their leave, and went on to the next compartment.

Our pilgrims now got busy trying to condense their real and innermost intentions to one infinitive clause, but were interrupted in this brain-cudgelling task when a young man entered the compartment at Rosenheim and took a seat next to the young enchantress. On taking off his coat, he was revealed as a young priest, indeed one newly ordained. He did not say so, of course, when he introduced himself as "Süss"; but an experienced nun can tell at a glance: that timid joy in his eyes, those thin cheeks under the smooth brow, his shy way of taking off his coat, blushing meanwhile to the roots of his hair at the piercing glances of so many people, and the unblemished blackness of his jacket, all these things could only proclaim a priest newly ordained, who still dwelt in the rarefied atmosphere of ordination, knowing as yet nothing of the oppressive fogs lurking in the vales of his profession. And here was Satan straightway setting him beside this serpent, this sophisticated Eve! Annaberta sighed, and set herself the task of keeping a watchful vigilance over this soul also. When the priest greeted his neighbor with excessive friendliness, the schoolteacher emitted a significant cough. Father Süss dropped his eyes in embarrassment. A mocking smile flashed over the face of the brimstone yellow. O wily Eve!

Once they had passed the border, two girls from the progressive parish youth group appeared, collected the envelopes, and took them to those in charge. Monsignor Schwiefele and Chaplain Schlüter were about to fall upon them in feverish inquisitiveness, but Birnmoser restrained them. "It is my job to evaluate the results. I'll read the answers out to you." Chaplain Schlüter was on the point of protesting most strongly at such cavalier treatment of the priesthood by a member of the laity, but he checked himself. He must hold his powers in reserve until they got to Rome, when he intended to inform the Holy Father, if possible in a private audience, of the improprieties prevalent in the Church, of the hierarchy's indolence, and of his own epoch-making ideas. "I shall lie doggo for these few days, and then I'll show you what

I'm made of," he thought, buttoning his coat up to the chin. "Perhaps we could read the most successful answers through the microphone, to distract the pilgrims a little?" suggested Monsignor Schwiefele. Birnmoser nodded.

And now, what were the pilgrims' main reasons for travelling to Rome? "To see the Holy Father." Naturally. "To kneel at the tomb of Saint Peter." "To feel the truly catholic nature of the Church." "To take a trip to Ostia." "To visit the seven basilicas." "To get to the south cheaply for once." ("What philistines such people are," growled the chaplain.) "To see the night life of a big city." ("Should we read that one through the loudspeakers as well?" asked Birnmoser. The chaplain nodded. "We mustn't cheat.") "That the Holy Father will bless me and I can write a nice essay afterwards."

"To see the catacombs and visit a business acquaintance." "To experience the singing of the liturgy by the Benedictines on the Aventino." ("Could be from the schoolmistress!") "To strengthen my faith, to bathe in the Mediterranean, and to stand face to face with the Apollo di Belvedere and the Venus di Lido." ("Don't read that one!" warned the monsignor. "Why not? It's a contemporary thought," riposted the chaplain. "Oh, all right," the monsignor sighed. He regretted now having agreed to the experiment.) "To visit my son's grave in Pomezia." Birnmoser plugged in a pause for emotion. "To pour out pure wine for the Holy Father." ("Only the chaplain can have written that," thought the monsignor.) "To breathe the air of classicism." "To learn to love the Church." ("Then you had better stay at home," grunted the chaplain.) "To buy some Vatican stamps and see the Colosseum." The monsignor agitated his arms, imploring them to switch off the microphone, the answers were growing more and more worldly. "Wait a bit, here's a very pious one: 'To get a lot of blessing for taking back to my orphan children and arrive home safely again with God's grace.' Isn't that nice?" "Bad grammar," cavilled the chaplain. "But good Catholicism," responded the monsignor, smiling to himself. That answer could only come from one person, and he knew who it was.

It was between Hall and Innsbruck that Sulamith

nudged her mother and whispered: "They're calling one another by their Christian names."

"Who are?"

"The priest and that girl. And her name is Eve."

"Sh, Suli. One doesn't say things like that." The schoolmistress laid a finger on her daughter's lips, then turned to the nun and whispered in her ear: "They are already using one another's Christian names, Father Süss and that Eve. Imagine, her name really is Eve. Very significant, is it not?"

Sister Annaberta nodded. What else could she do? She was, in fact, very sad at heart. She had imagined this journey to Rome as an unbroken chain of comfort and joy, and now here she was, floundering from one worry to another. She had just been wondering if Sister Glyceria would put too much sugar in the orphans' gruel, and now she was tormented about a young priest's spiritual welfare. It was evident the schoolmistress would have liked to embark on a malicious whispered conversation about "him" and "her," but Annaberta showed little inclination for it. She closed her eyes and prayed, first for the orphan children, then for the young priest, and finally for Eve too.

The train was thundering up towards the Brenner Pass. The parish youth club of both sexes, lowland born, flung open the windows, letting the wind stream through

their hair, and bellowed out a song to the gigantic Tyrol mountains: "At Mantua in durance vile the loyal Hofer[1] lay." On hearing of this the chaplain was horrified. He stormed through the carriages, treading on the toes of an aged dame en route, so that she squeaked pitiably, and at last reached the well-aired compartments of his flock, where he hectored them:

"What are you thinking of, screeching like that in front of open windows? Do you want to ruin your voices? I refuse to sing in front of the Holy Father with you if

[1] Andreas Hofer, the national hero of the Tyrol in the time of Napoleon.

you are hoarse." The argument took effect. Andreas Hofer was carried back to his grave. His native landscape, however, grew more and more lovely.

Sister Annaberta thought so too. Never before had she seen such mountains. She thought at times that the savage peaks must topple down upon the train, so steeply did they shoot up beside the track.

"In the long run, I should get scared living here," she remarked to Frau Raibeisen. "Our mountains at home are only children, with round humps, and not so high that you have to dislocate your neck to look up to them."

"You should thank God that you are able to live in a mountain district at all," countered the schoolmistress. "I have been banished to flat country, alas. Nothing to see, no museum, no natural beauty anywhere. And the young people are as stupid as the land is flat. Just imagine, in a town with practically twenty thousand inhabitants, there is not a soul I can recommend as a fit acquaintance for my daughter. I tell you, they're an unbelievably common crowd. And not a scrap of feeling for liturgy! Even my spiritual adviser refuses to believe that his pastoral methods are antiquated. Recently he boxed my sister-in-law's nephew on the ears while he was serving at Mass. Didn't he, Suli?" Her daughter nodded. "And the children are vile. Enough to make one scream. You should thank God, dear Sister, that you have nothing to do with children. I feel sure you work in the kitchen?"

"In an orphanage, ma'am."

"But—what? As a teacher?"

"No, no," parried Annaberta shyly. "There are twenty to thirty little orphan boys and girls, and I have to do what I can to take the place of their missing parents."

"Orphans. Isn't that frightfully unpleasant? I mean, I suppose it's not too bad when one knows who the parents were. But how often one doesn't! One can let oneself in for all sorts of ne'er-do-wells with criminal backgrounds. Just think how many lawbreakers come out of orphanages. Please, Sister, I don't mean your orphanage, naturally. But I expect it can't give you all that much pleasure."

"Not all that much, but it's enough."

"Oh well, so long as the children are young and sweet. But what about later on? That crowd doesn't know the meaning of the word gratitude. Or so I find with my pupils. And most of *those* are from good families. Only one out of eighty sent me news of her engagement. And I didn't learn she was married until after she was divorced."

"There I can't complain, ma'am. Our children are very faithful after they leave us. They paid for my trip to Rome, in fact." This remark made the schoolmistress visibly furious. "If only I had kept quiet," said Annaberta to herself, vowing in the future to be more sparing, more cautious with her words, so as not to offend anyone else.

"So you have never suffered any disappointments from your pupils?" the schoolmistress jealously probed.

"There are little disappointments every day," confessed the nun.

"And big ones, massive ones? You know what I mean."

"Those too."

The schoolmistress, seeming to find a certain consolation, unpacked a thick ham sandwich and shared it with her daughter. When the impoverished baroness saw this, she fingered a rusk out of her little handbag and stuffed half of it into her husband's mouth: "Chew thirty-two times, don't forget, Ferdinand."

"Brennero! Brennero!"

"How strange. Where I come from, we say '*feurio*' when there's a fire,"[1] observed Annaberta to the schoolmistress, thinking for the first time on the journey that she had said something sensible.

Sulamith began to giggle, the schoolmistress hid her face behind her handkerchief, the baroness nudged the baron, and the young priest bowed his head. Only Eve

[1] *Brennen* in German means "to burn."

man, one Hail Mary after another. The other occupants bothered less about correct pronunciation and keeping in time. And if here and there they swallowed a syllable, the response in their hearts was all the more clear.

"—and declared to her the incarnation of our Lord and Saviour . . ."

For miles around the countryside lay bathed in golden light, a token of farewell pouring from the sun in unstinting plenty. Wagons piled high with corn swayed like schooners across the rich green expanse. The world revolved in its Father's blessing. And all was enfolded in Mary's blue mantle.

"—understanding from the angel that her cousin, Saint Elisabeth, had conceived, went with haste into the mountains of Judea to visit her . . ."

"I wonder how far it is from Nazareth to Judea? Farther than from Munich to Rome? And there were no trains in those days, no monsignor or Herr Birnmoser to take care of everything. Mary and Joseph must have had an awfully long walk," Annaberta thought to herself. "Could I have managed it? I hardly think so. Even less, I imagine, Frau Raibeisen. If anyone from our compartment could, it'd most likely be the athletic young lady at the window . . ."

"—brought forth our Redeemer Jesus Christ at Bethlehem . . ."

"Half-past six. Now Sister Glyceria will be taking my

place, clapping her hands to call the twenty-six orphans in to supper, washing their little faces so that no earthly stains hinder their chirping of 'Jesus be praised' before they fall upon the tomato salad and the sweet cherries. Will the children miss me as much as I am missing them? Dear heaven, wouldn't it be wonderful to go to Rome with the children? Unfortunately that cannot be. But I promised to bring them all back a little present, a nice little present—"

"—on the day of her purification, presented the child Jesus in the temple . . ."

The little baron, who had been praying more and more softly, had now fallen fast asleep and was snuggled, open-mouthed, on his wife's bosom. The imposing dame

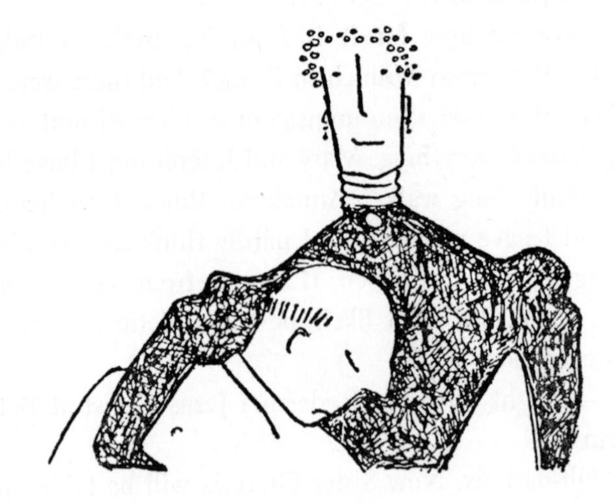

affectionately stroked his bald head as though he were her baby son, and motioned to the others to pray more quietly so that His Excellency would not wake up. "Good Lord," Annaberta thought, "Mary sacrificed her only son, and he can't even make the sacrifice of staying awake until the end of a rosary. Yet perhaps he's really tired, tired from hunger—tomorrow I'll slip a sausage sandwich into his pocket on the quiet . . ."

Then somebody in the center carriage must inadvertently have pressed the microphone switch, for suddenly the monsignor's voice blared through the loud-speaker: "Heart!" and "Ace!" from the mouth of the hop-farmer. The pious pilgrims were startled, those who had been asleep sat bolt upright, the schoolmistress reached for the communication cord. But good Annaberta just thought: "Oh, so they've finished their rosary already."

2. *Concerning the veiled charms of Florence, or why Sister Annaberta saw her gravestone in the night*

Goodness knows what the people of Florence had been up to in this year of grace, that their patron saint, John the Baptist, should, on his feast day, see fit to cast all the waters of Jordan at their heads and rooftops. Maybe the Florentines had deserved the penance—but our good German pilgrims refused to believe that they should suffer too. The sky had been cloudless the night before when they had entered their lodgings, dead beat from the long train journey but full of hope for a fine day on the morrow. And now Monsignor Schwiefele's flock, pious as lambs, patient as ewes, or wild as rams, according to their various temperaments, stood looking up at the damp, gray sky. All the rainclouds in Italy had made Tuscany their rendezvous. Florence, this flower among cities, was behaving like a proud and noble lady, who suffers herself to be admired only through a veil. The mood of the pilgrims at their spartan breakfast still oscillated between anger and hope. The weather forecast for the Apennine peninsula had, after all, spoken of sunshine, with rain only "at times." So this misery surely could not last. When someone gifted in mathematics reminded them that time could be long, indeed infinite, he was silenced with angry stares.

They set out therefore on a tour of the city with borrowed umbrellas. The leaders of the group had chosen the itinerary with care. Wise from long experience, the monsignor gave the Uffizzi and similar establishments a wide berth, lest the evidence of antiquity and the Renaissance might confuse the minds of Bavarian countrywomen and Swabian mail-guards. Their surprise at the number of satyrs and bacchantes tumbling about under the pinions of the Church came quite soon enough in Rome, where it could not be avoided. In Florence one could confidently do without such things, for with its churches and convents the city offered an excess of art, much more than could be digested in one morning by Germans avid for beauty.

In every church Annaberta assailed heaven, begging it to show a little consideration and to dole out to her sun-starved compatriots the ration of light and warmth

included in the cost of the pilgrimage, and which was necessary for its success. In vain. It was raining when they went into San Marco; it was raining when they came out of San Marco; it was raining when they stood before Michelangelo's David; it was raining when the chaplain explained Ghiberti's doors; it was raining in front of San Lorenzo and behind Santa Croce; it was raining on the Ponte Vecchio and at the Signoria; it rained all the morning and it rained all the afternoon, till the dirty river Arno swelled into a greasy yellow Yangtse.

Who, then, can wonder at our pilgrims' lamentable mood during dinner? And when Birnmoser attempted to console the wailing victims of the Florentines' sins by referring to the fine weather all over the rest of Italy, the pilgrims looked at him with murder in their eyes. It had in fact been possible for some hours to see through a telescope where the clouds ended in the west. But since they were moving from south to north, that did not help much. In any case, the opposition now moved in for a general attack. The grumblers began to smell all kinds of rats, carping at this and criticizing that. If one found the day's program too extended, another said it was too short. One lady complained that the food was oily, a second pronounced it too dry. Even the schoolmistress grew fractious and wanted to know why they had been kept out of the Uffizzi. Where was the monsignor eating, anyway? He was not to be found. With a Florentine prelate, perhaps? And this after he had promised to share every joy and every sorrow with his pilgrims. Men who at the Brenner Pass had joined together in praise of chianti began to long for their native beer, and swore to go back to Andechs for their next pilgrimage, it being cheaper and more healthy. Sulamith, in addition, resented the Florentine youths' impudent stares, and she was inconsolable until her mother explained that in Italy intelligent girls always stood out.

While young and old, male and female, were thus revelling in melancholy and giving themselves up to lamentation, the dark clouds slunk back into the Apennines like sated wolves, granting to the evening sun a late mastery of Florence. This city of genius, city of the Muses, was not destined to remain in the pilgrims' memory as a place of borrowed umbrellas and mud-flecked trousers.

Sister Annaberta was the first to notice the transformation in the heavens. "So it was not in vain after all," she murmured to herself. Her neighbor, Baroness Neuhaus, thought she meant the grumbling. Oh, child of the world!

Like a magic wand, the shafts of sunlight awakened in the pilgrims a spirit of enterprise. The official program was relaxed, and each was allowed to seek happiness in his or her own way. Quick to make up her mind as she always was, the baroness invited the nun for a short stroll. She ordered her husband to come along, and not to think of going out with one of the younger ladies. He obeyed. Florence was glittering in a sea of gold. The raindrops on the branches shone like jewels, the city's damp rooftops gleamed like silver plate.

"We'll go to the Piazzale Michelangelo. You can get

a most beautiful view over the city from there," said Baroness Neuhaus, leading the way. She was quite right. The sister stared enraptured upon the city lying at her feet, across to the mountains, and into the shimmering

west. The impoverished aristocrat stood on tiptoe with excitement:

"Look, Sister, at this majestic city, enjoy it, let its sublimity pour through you! It dared to defy emperors and kings; to the worldly rich it lent money on interest; artists shone like sunflowers in the garden of its talents! All these proud campaniles, with the dome of the Brunelleschi out there in front, do they not give it an absolutely heroic air? Oh, if only you could feel, as I do, the genius of this city, cradle of the Renaissance, womb of the modern world! And look up there, where Fiesole beckons—the very name is music! This is culture, a chiselled landscape, strength given form, beauty in restraint! The most lamentable cypress-tree, the most neglected garden wall proclaims its nobility!" The good baron would probably have continued for some time in this enthusiasm (moreover to the great joy of our sister) had not the baroness thrust into the wheel of his poetry the spoke of her prose: "And how do you proclaim your nobility? By putting the wrong socks on. The mouse-gray ones don't go with that brown jacket. How many more times must I tell you?"

Then they went rather quickly down, crossed the Arno and entered the heart of the city. All Florence was out enjoying the mild evening. Sister Annaberta remained faithfully by the baron's side, as though she wished him to understand that for her his inspired words had not fallen on stony ground, as in his wife's case. But where was his wife, anyway?

"She is sure to be looking in the shop windows. It has become a passion of hers, now that we have no money."

"Oh, I love doing that too. I'm always so glad when I see so many things I don't need. Then I feel like a king," said Annaberta.

"We ought actually to wait for her. But then we should never move from this spot. And we do want to enjoy the evening air a little, do we not?"

"Will your wife be able to find her way back to where we're staying?"

"Better than we can. She knows a few phrases of Italian."

"What about us?"

"Don't worry, dear Sister. We shall look for the cathedral. I know my way back from there." The baron was now speaking with complete assurance. His wife's departure had aroused his self-confidence. He seemed a changed man, so much so that this curious pair relaxed into a cheerful conversation, so cheerful that they were completely unaware that they were being slowly absorbed into a vast crowd of people. It was not until these people formed up in ranks and began to sing that the baron stopped in his tracks; "What have we got into?"

"A procession," Annaberta affirmed. "It must be in honor of Saint John, the patron saint. Otherwise there wouldn't be so many people."

"Then I don't mind. The procession can only be going to the cathedral or Santa Croce. I know my way home from both of them. The best thing we can do is go along with it." So they joined the ranks. Those marching beside them cast somewhat hostile glances at the two foreigners; and two urchins pulled faces. Annaberta nodded amiably on all sides, and then strove to concentrate on her devotions. She felt splendid. A nun is always more at home in a procession than in a yawning mob of tourists. And how energetically the people were singing! It was a pity she did not understand the words, they sounded so inspired. And how many men there were taking part! That would have been something for those at home to see! For this was Christianity as it originally was, and not something reserved for old women.

The procession was so long that they could see nothing of the saint or the priests. They were walking at the end of the line, and her view to the front was blocked by the angular heads before her. The pace quickened, the singing grew louder, wilder, almost a scream. The head of the procession suddenly came to a halt. A jolt ran through its ranks. Those at the back, however, soon started pushing forward, and interrupted their singing to roar: "Avanti, fratelli, avanti." "Avanti, viva!" Annaberta joined in with enthusiasm, thinking this meant something like "For ever and ever, amen." A man on her right, daubed with oil and soot, clapped her hard on the shoulder: "Bravo, Suora! Avanti! Per un mondo migliore! Avanti!"

Then came shrill whistles, sirens wailed, the whole crowd ran forward, back, turned in on itself, struggled and fanned out, shrieking in turmoil, waving hats, clenching fists. The baron turned pale.

"Don't be afraid, sir! It's nothing but southern piety. I've read about it in the diocesan magazine. They'll be giving the Blessing at any moment." But before Annaberta could enlarge any further on what she had learned from the diocesan magazine, her words were drowned in a howl of rage from the mob; cursing and raving, people leaped to the sides of the road, scuttling into the houses, and Annaberta, horrified, had no time to think before steel-helmeted policemen were charging at them with long hosepipes.

"Hoses!" screamed the baron, and he tried to drag the nun to the safety of the pavement. Too late. The raging jets of authority had already caught her, and they did not let her go until she was drenched from her wimple to her sandals (and the baron from his bald head to his ankles).

When the hot-headed guardians of law and order realized what peaceable passers-by had strayed in front of their hoses, they expressed their regret, offering to drive the signor and the suora back to their lodgings in a police car.

So the signor and the suora crept into the car.

"I think we got ourselves mixed up in a communist demonstration," said the baron, downcast.

"I think we did," was Annaberta's response.

"I should never have thought there were so many communists in Florence. The city looks so Christian."

"So Christian, sir."

"Of course, now I remember: in Italy as a whole, a third of the population is communist."

"A third? But then, the revolution might break out any day."

"Very possibly, Sister. Only recently, the Government discovered some large stocks of weapons."

The police car was crossing the Arno.

"I could throw myself in the river," wailed the baron. "What a blunder! Imagine us not noticing anything wrong."

"I had seen a red flag. But it was so like the flag of our girls' club that I thought nothing of it, fool that I am," said Annaberta, striking her forehead.

"Fool that *I* am," rejoined the baron. "You need not only blame yourself. But I, dear Sister, am threatened with a storm, in comparison with which that hose was a mere drizzle."

The poor creature, Annaberta mused. All his chosen eloquence will not save him from his wife's bad temper. Such, then, are the trials of wedlock!

The tourists crowded goggle-eyed into the hotel lobby as the police car drew up and "spat out" the two demonstrators, as the baron put it. That was in any case the last word he spoke that evening; his wife immediately grabbed him by his damp collar and, ominously silent, hustled him to their room.

To avoid catching a cold—for she must not be ill in Rome!—Sister Annaberta went straight to bed. Her room had a balcony outside. There, her habit swung to and fro, drying in the mild evening air. She had begged an iron from the hotel management, so that early the next morning she could restore her dried-out habit to its prescribed neatness.

For the schoolmistress it was still too early to sleep, so she drew a chair up to the sister's bed and passed on her latest observations.

"Where do you think the parish youth club members are? In the amusement park! And the chaplain still not back. Did you ever hear anything like it? They might at least have invited Sulamith along. The poor girl has got nothing out of this journey so far. Of course, I wouldn't have let her go with them. In any case, as soon as I get back, I shall report Chaplain Schlüter's dubious behavior to the Archbishop. I most certainly shall. And the newly ordained Father Süss? Every bit as bad, the sanctimonious hypocrite. Suli discovered him in the Café Trieste with his dolled-up travelling companion."

"In the Gelateria Medici, Mummy," her daughter corrected her, "Herr Birnmoser was in the Café Trieste, with an Italian girl."

"Thank you very much; it's a good thing you reminded me. Just imagine it, Sister. And *they* are supposed to be in charge of us. We must take care that in the future there are no gaps in the program, so that vice will not stand a chance. I have quite a few connections in the diocese. My sister-in-law's sister is Canon Windelband's housekeeeper's niece. I shall exert my influence so that pilgrimages really are pilgrimages. I wager not a tenth of all those ladies and gentlemen travelling to Rome today in coaches and special trains would, in the Middle Ages, have been prepared to walk there on foot, let alone to Lourdes or Fatima. What do you think, Sister?"

"Nothing at all, Mummy," came Suli's frigid interruption. "She will be snoring in a minute."

Furious, the schoolmistress rose, "Asleep, is she? She may be pious—but she has absolutely no manners." And with this pronouncement she swept, followed by her daughter, from the room.

But Annaberta was not left on her own. Fra Angelico's angels, with golden hair and glittering robes, thronged round her bed and, having brought their harps and trumpets with them, blew celestial music in her ears. Perhaps they blew a little too loudly; for when the sister awoke, it was still not yet eleven o'clock. Yet she felt so much better that she decided to iron her habit right away, if it was dry. And it was, almost. Annaberta carried it back into the room, plugged in the electric iron, and lowered the venetian blinds, for she wanted no peeping Toms at her evening work. The iron took half a rosary to get hot enough. Then, humming a canticle, she began to press her skirt into its regulation folds.

The silence of the night was suddenly shattered by a wild crackling sound. Annaberta started. Was that machine-guns? And now explosions—bombs, no doubt!

And cries in the distance. "One-third communist. The revolution might break out any day"—she herself had said this to Baron Neuhaus that very evening. Were her fears coming true? Were the communists, driven to breaking-point by the failure of their demonstration, seizing power? Was this the revolution?

More firing, explosions, cries of triumph—probably the bridges were being blown to pieces, the lovely Ponte Vecchio! The mob will soon be streaming through the streets, "as women grow like wild hyenas, making of horror their sport"[1]—Alas, was there any point in hiding or screaming for help? Sister Annaberta, who normally had never been daunted by a mad dog, a Community Group Leader, or an enraged wild boar, did not now dare to take one courageous step out onto the balcony or the landing; indeed she did not even venture to draw up the blinds. The hotel was suspiciously silent. Did the pilgrims not realize what was happening, or had they all crept terrified into the cellar? Or had they fled the city, helter-skelter? The shooting and the noise was coming closer and closer. It will not be long now before the revolutionaries get to the hotel. Will foreigners be spared? The laity, perhaps. For her, the monsignor, the chaplain and young Father Süss, their German nationality will certainly not save them from prison, or worse.

[1] Schiller: *Das Lied von der Glocke.*

And it was strange that of the three priests travelling with the group, although she had liked the chaplain least, it was him she could best imagine in the role of a martyr. The monsignor would probably make a much less heroic figure, especially if it occurred to his murderers to roast him alive on a grill, like his patron, Saint Lawrence.

Revolution—so that was why she had had those sinister forebodings previous to her journey! And Sister Felicity had laughed at her. Will she weep when she learns of this sad end? Of course she will. And the children even more.

A fiery red light was already flickering through the Venetian blinds, the rattle of guns was growing more and more violent, the cries of triumph wilder and wilder. Here they come, Satan's henchmen, the godless Muscovites! Lo, there was a bang on the door, and another, and another—

Sister Annaberta, family name Vogelwieser, stood up straight as a church candle, resolved not to let herself be stabbed from behind, but to dab her hot iron on the face of her first attacker and to defend her life to the last sigh.

"Come in," she cried, in a sudden burst of courage.

But the door opened a mere fraction. And Sulamith's voice whispered: "Do come out on the veranda, Sister. You mustn't miss this. The people of Florence are giving a firework display in honor of their patron saint, and you've never seen anything like it."

Sister Annaberta seldom dreamed. Yet that night her own gravestone appeared to her, in the shape of an iron, and on it was the inscription:

Here lies Sister Annaberta
Virgin and Martyr
Requiescat in pace

3. *Concerning the first walk through Rome, or how first the sister's worries about Eve, and then the electric razor, were taken from her*

"Roma aeterna, Roma aeterna, Roma aeterna," chanted the wheels as the train thundered through the Tiber valley, and the pilgrims pressed their noses flat against the windows, each hoping to be the first to make out the dome of Saint Peter's. At last came the cry of deliverance: "There it is! There it is!"

Everyone sprang up, only Sister Annaberta staying in her seat. She had said little since Florence. She was unwilling to relax her tense expectation in idle chatter. But only a few minutes now remain, and then she will tread the ground of the Eternal City. How often she had dreamed of this moment, longed for its arrival—and now the gratitude of former orphans had made this great joy possible for her, for her alone, she who yet of all her sisters was certainly the least deserving. (So she thought.)

Gigantic tenements glided past the window, then a long cemetery wall. The rails galloped by in ever-increasing numbers, the train braked, and finally stood still: Stazione Termini.

No pilgrim bent down to kiss the earth. They all had quite enough trouble keeping their bits and pieces together and fighting their way unharmed through the crush. The monsignor sweated with responsibility. The sweat, however, paid off; all his lambs got to the station entrance hall in one piece, the baron alone having suffered the loss of his purse. That was, thank God, a minor sacrifice. His wife, in any case, looked after all large sums of money. Then they were taken by coach to their lodgings. On arrival, the pilgrims sank exhausted on their beds, with the exception of Fräulein Emerenz Obermair who, being a pilgrim of some experience, first searched her bed thoroughly for bugs. But not one of these clinging little creatures, which are as hard to get away from in places of pilgrimage as sugar rosaries, was to be found.

As it was already nearly four o'clock in the afternoon and stifling hot into the bargain, those in charge of the group had arranged no excursions, but proposed bed for all. Whoever felt like it could of course go out independently for a stroll through the city. The monsignor, however, warned them against doing so; for in the past, many a pilgrim had gone astray in Rome and disappeared, never to be seen again.

A terrible thought! But it did not deter Annaberta from making the most of this opportunity to carry out an intention she had. What intention? Well, she asked Birnmoser, did he know the mother house of the Fathers of the Holy Cross? Birnmoser did, and he immediately offered to accompany the sister there. Eve, who happened to pass by at that moment, said a private stroll through Rome was just what she wanted, and if the lady and gentleman had no objection, she would love to join them. How could the gallant Birnmoser have any objection to providing Eve with her first impressions of the Eternal City? There was much that Sister Annaberta could have said against such a scheme; but she was too modest to impose a veto. So the two children of this world put the sister between them, and they set out. Sister Annaberta had but seldom known the honor of walking in the middle. This time, however, she found it an advantage on moral grounds, since it was vital to protect the good Birnmoser against the brimstone yellow's machinations. Birnmoser was presumably a married man with several children; but according to what Sister Felicity had said, the possession of children does not guard a man against folly.

Out in the street, the sister was almost stunned by the sheer volume of traffic. Bicycle bells tinkled, brakes squealed, motor horns blared, people cursed—and all this in the heart of Christendom! She would never have got across the street unaided. Birnmoser, however, led her with majestic calm across the busiest streets and squares, a guardian angel could not have done it better.

"That huge church in front of us is the Lateran," he explained. "We shall get a closer look later on. It is consecrated to Saint John the Baptist, whose head reposes under the high altar."

"You will find it difficult to prove that, my dear Herr Birnmoser," the chestnut-haired girl let fall. "Most probably it is the skull of a Moslem who was beheaded, and which his fellow countrymen sold for a handful of silver to some naïve crusader."

For some seconds, Sister Annaberta's heart stood still. What blasphemy! But these well-read women are all alike, shameless and godless. Birnmoser too seemed angered by his fair companion's rationalistic attitude; at any rate he did not venture to say anything about the so-called Holy Steps.

A narrow street of shops led through to the Colosseum. Eve became very interested in all those that had clothes in the windows. Birnmoser's inborn chivalry would not allow him to leave her standing there and walk on with Annaberta. He could not, however, stifle the observation that he, thank goodness, did not need to plague himself with such worries.

"Not you," parried Eve, "but what about your wife?"

"I'm not married," he confessed, to both his companions' astonishment. "I travel about too much to be able to devote myself to a wife."

"That's strange," Eve riposted cunningly, "I can never travel about enough for my liking."

Their entrance into the vast oval of the Colosseum put an end, thank goodness, to this insidious dialogue. The sister was overwhelmed to think she was standing where Saint Peter and many thousands of martyrs had died. She had to sit down. Birnmoser meanwhile painted in heartfelt words an impressive picture of the countless Christian victims that had here fought the lions, jeered at by emperor and mob, strengthened with visions of heaven. Ankle-deep had their murderers waded in that blood which had become the seeds of the Church. Birnmoser paused, as if in expectation of a critical remark from the young lady. But this time she too was silent.

Not for long, of course. By the time they got to the basilica of Maxentius she was considerably devaluating Birnmoser's assertions. Historical research, she said, could find evidence of a mere three hundred Roman martyrdoms. That meant an average of one martyr per year for the period from Nero to Constantine. Birnmoser ought now to have been really angry at her way of undermining his authority. Unfortunately, he was no longer capable of being so.

The mother house they were seeking was situated not far from the communist headquarters in the Via dei Botteghe Oscure—the street of dark shops.

"What a superb Renaissance building," remarked Eve with enthusiasm.

"What a stuffy great box," thought the nun. "No garden, no playground, no chicken-run—how can one serve God in such a place?"

Whom did she wish to see, asked Birnmoser.

"The Superior General, preferably."

That would not be easy. He would see if it were possible. Was it an important matter, then?

"Most important."

"In the name of God, in that case," said Birnmoser, disappearing into the porter's lodge.

Sister Annaberta was left alone with the girl. Now was the chance to call her attention to her improper behavior towards the newly ordained priest, she said to herself. It was, after all, part of a nun's duty.

"Might I ask you a question, Miss—?" she began

most diplomatically, "Miss— I'm afraid I don't know your name."

"Eve Süss, student of medicine," answered she.

"Süss—?" Annaberta started with surprise. "Then, Miss, you must be related to the reverend young gentleman?"

"If you care to put it that way: I am his sister," said Eve with a smile. "I hope that occurred to you straight away."

"Not straight away, no," Annaberta candidly admitted.

"You wanted to ask me something," Fräulein Süss reminded her after a pause.

"Oh, yes—I wanted to ask you, er, I wanted to ask you—why are you so sceptical about all relics?"

"Not about all of them, but of a great many. Maybe I should never have studied anatomy. One reaches a point of no return. And now I have to drag my scepticism around with me as many unfortunate souls do their superstitions. But here comes our escort. Well, how did it go with the rector?"

"All right," Birnmoser announced, half in pleasure and half-annoyed, for he had had to tip the porter heavily, and haggle with a couple of "assistant rectors." "Suora Annaberta, the Superior General is waiting for you."

"The Superior General is waiting for me." Sister Annaberta smoothed her habit, tweaked her wimple into place, then marched straight as a die towards the bronze doors, where she was received by a white-robed monk.

The mother houses of the Papacy's various divisions are as alike as military H.Q.s. When you know one, you know your way about in all of them. The whole building is a labyrinth of gloomy corridors. Bare walls exude asceticism. High windows, blind with the dust of centuries, vouchsafe only brief glimpses of the inner courtyard, where a fountain struggles in vain to combat the paralyzing solemnity of its environment. Latin texts writhe above the doors, the smell of garlic mingles with the fumes of incense. And from a guest cell there escapes a solitary whiff of tobacco, which flutters off helplessly through the gloom.

"What a lot of things must be against the rules here!" was Annaberta's only thought as, accompanied by the white friar as if by a shadow, she walked the long, long way to the audience room. Her eyes could make out only the vague outlines of this chamber. Here too, the daylight was repulsed by purple curtains, while inch-thick carpets swallowed up every unwanted sound. The walls were decorated with the gigantic portraits of dignitaries, whose period of office had robbed them of the power to smile. Sister Annaberta had up to now imagined God's Church as a garden; fenced, it is true, but gay and sunny—now she stood drastically corrected. What little was left of her self-confidence melted away like the candles of Corpus Christi in hot June sunshine. And she was supposed to negotiate with a prince of the Church in this setting?

There passed some minutes of respectful waiting. At last a double door opened, and two men entered, also wearing flowing white robes. Disappointment flashed over their faces as they caught sight of the insignificant nun. Had Birnmoser perhaps announced an abbess of royal blood, or a mother superior loaded with dollars?

The smaller of the two turned out to be an interpreter,

and he requested the supplicant to state her business, bearing in mind that the most reverend Superior General's every moment was precious, poised as he was for a long journey.

Sister Annaberta dropped a most submissive curtsy and asked if the reverend father was acquainted with a certain Father Toni—sorry, Father Timotheus Stangl.

"Of course," came the somewhat tart reply; "Father Timotheus was in Africa."

"Not any more. For two years he has been in Cholapur, India," Sister Annaberta reminded him.

The interpreter shrugged his shoulders up to his ears, implying that the sister need not take it upon herself to correct the most reverend father a second time.

"Yes, quite correct, Cholapur," the latter meanwhile confirmed.

"Father Timotheus is one of my orphans. He was the first I had to make his way into the priesthood, and he has always been particularly faithful. That is why I want to give him something. Could the most reverend father rector see that Toni—sorry, Timotheus, receives the present, and secondly, that he is allowed to keep it?"

If it were not too large he would take it himself, the Superior General answered, he was flying to Madras in a few hours.

It was just an electric razor, stated Annaberta.

All right, then, he would have plenty of room for it in his travelling-bag, said the rector with a smile. Had she any other request?

"That Toni may keep it. He has a very strong beard. Even when he was fifteen he had to shave every fortnight. Oh, dear, what a torment *that* was for both of us!"

The Superior General smiled once more, stretched out his ring for her to kiss, and blessed her. The white-robed monk appeared at the door again. The sister followed him, exultant. She now knew that Toni would be given her present in a few days. But she was suddenly overcome with anxiety; what if his jungle mission house was not connected to an electricity supply? Was that, perhaps, why the interpreter had laughed so disdainfully?

The Superior General, meanwhile, gazed, musing, after the nun.

"Simple creatures, these nuns," said the interpreter, displeased, hoping to have guessed his superior's thoughts. The latter, however, shook his head brusquely, and with a severe expression on his face pressed his index finger to his brother's lips, silencing them.

Towards the end of her wordless march, Annaberta quickened her pace, partly for joy that the audience had been successful, but also because she was concerned for the moral safety of the pair she had left outside. But she need not have worried: they were standing on opposite sides of the street, Birnmoser studying a newspaper and Eve a hat-shop window, with the roaring traffic between them.

"Did you quarrel?" asked Annaberta, full of hope.

Birnmoser shook his head despondently.

4. *Concerning the fountain of life, or why that night they all sank dead tired into slumber*

As faithful sons and daughters of the Church—and that they all were, from Luitpold the sacristan to the robust chaplain from Kohlenpott—their first goal next day could be none other than Saint Peter's (or San Pietro, according to the schoolmistress). The Roman sky was in its most gracious mood. Cheerful and in high spirits, the pilgrims clambered into their blue coaches, forgetting even that their breakfast coffee had been unsweetened. The only difference of opinion was yet another altercation between the monsignor and the chaplain. Both, unfortunately, thought it meet that a hymn should be sung on this last lap of the pilgrimage. And of course, each made a different choice. The chaplain dismissed "Gentle Queen of Heaven" as late-romantic slush, and the monsignor "The Hour is nigh" as a youthful aberration. By the time a compromise had been reached and both launched out into "A House of Glory," the buses were already swinging into the Via della Conciliazione.

"It's not worth it now," said the monsignor, making signs for the singing to stop, "we shall be at Saint Peter's Square before we reach the chorus."

The Italian drivers must have thought they had been hired for a Jewish school's summer treat, so wild and enthusiastically did those normally decried for their Teutonic coldness behave when the façade of Saint Peter's appeared, gleaming bright in the morning sun. Scarcely had they climbed down from the coaches before the progressive youth club members of both sexes were streaming across the majestic square, their banners and coats flying out behind them, looking neither to the left nor the right, past the obelisk, racing towards the doorway and up those broad, solemn steps which were created for a measured, devout tread—Sister Annaberta's, for example. She, though her heart was pounding ever more wildly, checked her impatient longing. Saint Peter's would not run away. She wanted to enjoy for as long as she could the delight that flooded her soul as she moved now so close to the goal of her earthly desires. Who knows what may come afterwards?

What came afterwards was disappointment. If someone recently dead knocked at the gate of paradise in expectation of all the bliss of heaven, and on entering found not exultant angelic choirs, but yawning boy scouts, Baedeker-studying Englishwomen and babbling clerics, he could hardly be more disappointed than was our sister at that moment. At the door she had taken a deep breath, to bear with fortitude the expected heavenly splendor—and now, instead of finding herself in a house of God, she stood in a show-room so vast that her head swam, she was surrounded not by a congregation at prayer, but by a kind of muted railway station coming and going: not a soul joined his hands to pray; people were either pointing eagerly into the air, or tapping the marble, or thumbing through their guide books. Even the monsignor (with what devotion he had celebrated the holy sacrifice that morning!) did not genuflect (was there even a vigil lamp alight anywhere?) but plunged straight into his lecture on the size of the church, the men who had built it, its artists, and so forth. Then with a great many "Ohs" and "Ahs," the group of pilgrims embarked on a tour of the side aisles and visited the papal tombs, which were higher than St. Mary's column in Munich.

Annaberta stayed true to her fellow pilgrims for ten minutes, and no more. Then she made her own way to the Confessio. But there also, tourists were chattering, this time in French. She looked round in despair: was there no corner here in which to pray?

Then she caught sight of the mighty dome above her head. Yes, if only she were up there! Then the people would look like ants crawling on the floor below, and their blasé chatter would sound like the whispering of seraphim. Up there one could pray! But she had not as yet sprouted wings of her own, she was still a lump of clay, fashioned in Adam's likeness. So she absent-mindedly said an Our Father at St. Peter's tomb, and then stumped disconsolately towards the exit. The monsignor intended to devote a whole hour to his conducted tour of Saint Peter's. She therefore had plenty of time to sit down outside. Her only hope was that a second visit to this gigantic church might make her feel a little more at home in it.

On coming out of the porch, she passed her hand over her brow in amazement. Oh God, what a lovely square! The wide oval lay drenched in sunshine, and around it, Bernini's columns stood like unmoving sentries. Above, a myriad chords rang from the deep blue bell of the Roman sky. And how calm it was, with the gentle breeze carrying away all the chatter and the questions and the answers. Annaberta walked slowly down the steps and leaned against a pillar not far from the left-hand fountain. The warm stone did her back good. She sat down to contemplate the tranquil scene. An old man lay having a morning nap, a weatherbeaten hat tilted over his face. A young woman sat rocking her little daughter in her arms, humming a tune. Three boys, brown-skinned and fuzzy-haired, like the nodding heathen children on the offertory box at home, were vigorously playing dice. Two slit-eyed clerics with crimson sashes were immersed in their breviaries. Her patient gaze took in all this until it was held by the fountain. This splendid fountain! Tirelessly, ceaselessly, it shot its jets of flashing silver up toward heaven, purest white and delicate blue joining in lively sport before the water plunged in joyful spray back into the huge basins to prepare for a fresh assault. What the lifeless pomp of Saint Peter's had failed to do was achieved by this

fountain: for the little nun from the orphanage in the Bavarian forest it became a symbol of the Church. There too, did not the fountain of grace tirelessly, ceaselessly well up and pour back, shot through with purest light, into white vessels? And though unfavorable winds may deflect its course, though millions of iridescent drops may fall on sterile pavements—the fountain is not avaricious of its bounty, it splashes and foams all the more proudly upwards.

"If only my orphans were with me," murmured the sister, almost bemused with so much splendor and such solemn thoughts. And then she prayed for the orphans, who were probably plundering the cherry-trees at that moment, for her travel companions, then standing before the cold forms of Canova's lamenting angels, for the lazybones lying yonder in the sun and the woman humming, for the fuzzy-haired children and the slit-eyed clerics with their crimson sashes; and she prayed that all might recognize in the Church the living fountain under God's open sky, and not the lifeless pomp of a vanished age.

The hour in Saint Peter's Square passed all too quickly. When Monsignor Schwiefele discovered the sister by the colonnade, he was seriously displeased; no one, he reminded her, was allowed to go her own way in Rome, since he could not afford to waste time searching for lost sheep; and it was imperative to keep conscientiously to the schedule. Chaplain Schlüter underlined this by remarking that one must show these Italians what was meant by German punctuality. The Italians, meanwhile, were certainly showing these Germans what was meant by nonchalance. The drivers were still lounging in the nearest espresso bar, calmly filling out Toto tickets.

At last they were ready to leave. The prearranged schedule went off without a hitch. The next stop was the Janiculum. Everyone out of the coaches to enjoy the view! Into the coaches again. Helter-skelter down, past the Fontana Paola, to Trastevere.

"I shouldn't like to get lost in this maze of streets," said Annaberta to the schoolmistress, who was sitting next to her.

"That would certainly be ill-advised. Even in ancient times, this Trastevere was a district of ill repute. The people here had their own moral codex, and even their own dialect." Which for this fanatical *précieuse* was no doubt a capital crime.

Before Annaberta had puzzled out what a moral codex might be, came once more the command: "Everyone out!" Santa Maria in Trastevere. Eyes dazzled by the glaring sunshine could make out little of the beautiful mosaics in this gloomy church. Five minutes later:

"Back to the coaches!" Santa Cecilia. Out of the coaches. A scant description of the church from Birnmoser, the parish youth group warbled a round in honor of the patron saint of music. Sister Annaberta said three Aves for Sister Cecilia, as she had promised she would. And back to the coaches again, over the Tiber—"Ladies and gentlemen, here the history of the world used to wash its feet"—past Santa Maria in Cosmedin and the Mouth of Truth. To the left, the ruins of the Palatine—"They're taking a long time to rebuild that!"—to the right, a desolate tract of land, the Circus Maximus. The way to the city walls built by Aurelian leads through the impressive Passeggiata Archeologica. Birnmoser pointed out a tiny church, San Giovanni in Olio, where the Saviour's favorite disciple had been flung into a vat of boiling oil, and miraculously emerged unharmed. Annaberta cast a timorous glance towards Eve the rationalist. But this time Eve kept her ideas to herself. And then began the Via Appia. Could that ever have been an imperial highway, that narrow lane flanked with old walls? The young men were disappointed, for they had expected a kind of antique motorway.

"Everyone out for the catacombs," ordered the monsignor. It was pleasant to have to cover the last stage of this journey on foot. Sister Annaberta had been secretly afraid that motorization might have encroached upon the underground city. She was very glad to see lovely gardens laid out above the catacombs. It was so exactly like her conception of death.

Birnmoser now bought a small wax candle for each pilgrim, and hired a German-speaking guide; then he and the chaplain led the way into the bowels of the earth. And not even here could the schoolmistress keep her intellectual superiority to herself. She kept, unfortunately, walking either directly behind or directly in front of Annaberta, and considered it her duty to enlighten the sister on all the guide's grammatical mistakes and on all the historical inaccuracies of his explanation. The sister at first fought in vain to achieve the pious state of mind that the occasion demanded, and it was some time before the proximity of so many holy tombs blunted her annoyance with the schoolmistress.

The pilgrims walked for nearly an hour through the murky corridors. No one had imagined the catacombs could be so extensive. When they were told that this underground city went down five storeys deep into the earth, and that there were catacombs not only here on the Via Appia, but also on all the arterial roads, only then did they realize what is involved when the Church has to work in secret, and thus renounce everything that makes it attractive to the senses. And suddenly something happened that had not been planned. While the pilgrims stood, silent and deeply moved, Chaplain

Schlüter urged them to pray for the persecuted Church of our own time, which had not even catacombs in which to take refuge, and which was compelled to fight an enemy compared with whom Nero and Diocletian were mere amateurs, an enemy who used not only physical torment as its weapon, but also spiritual annihilation and the corrosive poison of propaganda. And thus they all prayed, loud and clear, that the light of faith and hope might not grow dim for their persecuted brethren, but shine out like the wax candles burning here in the catacombs.

The sound of the Lord's Prayer died away. The joined hands were loosed. Then Monsignor Schwiefele stepped up to the chaplain, stretched out his right hand—with his left he furtively wiped his eyes—and said,

"Now we have reached *one* goal on our pilgrimage. May God reward you for it, brother."

"Amen," rang out in a bass voice as deep as the five storeys of the catacombs. Everyone turned smiling to see who had spoken. It was the hop-farmer, who now fingered his moustache in embarrassment. "Sorry 'bout that," he said.

"But why?" answered Birnmoser. "You only thought out loud what we were all thinking to ourselves."

On reaching the light of day once more, Sulamith quoted: "A tear is shed, and earth receives us back,"[1]

[1] Goethe.

thus earning for herself respectful glances from the older ladies. The sacristan muttered that the catacombs would be nicer if they didn't smell like a cellar full of potatoes, thus garnering for himself a look of disapproval from Sister Annaberta. She would have liked most of all to go back down alone, to keep a little longer in her heart this feeling of intense piety. But the drivers were already sounding their horns, as though every second's delay were being deducted from their salary. The chaplain looked at his watch:

"What's the matter with these neurotic people? We are only a minute late."

"What do you expect, Father? The Italians are a talented race. They have learned punctuality from us too quickly for our liking," Eve roguishly observed, thus attracting to herself the abhorrence of the whole parish youth group.

Our German troop was storming ten minutes later through the pleasant atrium of the basilica of Saint Paul without the Walls. Deeply impressed by this church's calm beauty, and equipped with postcards of the picturesque abbey cloisters, on they went past the pyramid of Cestius—"How I should have loved to visit the tomb of Goethe's son!" cried the schoolmistress—and up to the Aventine.

The Aventine, a plebeian quarter in ancient Rome, is

today a quiet residential district. And no pilgrim was surprised to learn that two noble orders rule here, the Benedictines and the Dominicans. They first peeped into the bright sanctuary of Santa Sabina, then had a second, more intensive look through the keyhole in the Square of the Knights of Malta. Here you can do openly what every mother tells her child not to. By the time everyone had enjoyed this housemaid's-eye-view of Saint Peter's dome, a thick cloud, gray as the capes of the Lateran Canons, had rolled up to unload itself right above the Aventine, indeed with such vehemence that the monsignor could do no other than shepherd his flock under that roofed pen of Saint Benedict, the church of San Anselmo, to keep them dry.

No provision had been made in the official program for a visit to this church, and so even Birnmoser was unable to say much about it. The rain drummed not only upon the roof, but also, since it obviously leaked, on the mosaic floor. Hey-ho, what a splishing and splashing, as though ultra-Catholic baroque cherubim were flitting round the rafters, showing their dislike of the church's sober interior by pelting it with stones. A monk, red in the face with exertion, was bringing out jam-pots to collect the deluge. Other monks, meanwhile, came out for a choir practice. With heavy books in their hands they gazed, now attentive, now fierce, at a confrere, obviously the cantor, who like a butterfly drunk on nectar fluttered between throne and altar, from one side of the choir to the other, exhorting the sons of Saint Benedict with many an imploring gesture to sing *più alto.*

Our pilgrims, who felt much refreshed by the shower of rain, watched in amusement the obstinate duel be-

tween the intonating cantor and the detonating monks. At last the cantor thought he had won (or was he giving up the struggle? No matter) and declared the practice over. The monks, who were more than a hundred in number, rose, bowed deeply, and left the choir in a procession so solemn that they might have been practicing not an Alleluia, but the De Profundis. A few of the younger ones, it is true, did not assume that expression of face one would expect from an order more than a thousand years old, but nodded amicably across to the group of pilgrims. Annaberta found this particularly distressing, and she racked her brains too, wondering why it was necessary to practice so much in order to sing in tune with the heavenly Alleluia.

The jam-pots had meanwhile overflowed. The rain began to slacken. Into the coaches, then, and off we go. "Who said something about being hungry? We are pilgrims, my friends. Think what the Roman martyrs endured—and you want to go on strike because your stomach is rumbling? Especially when we are about to enjoy something absolutely first-rate: the Colosseum." All right, then! Down the Aventine, past the strange obelisk, out of the coaches, into the Colosseum. The girls regret not being able to see it by moonlight. The boys clamber up to the topmost gallery and take snaps by the yard. The monsignor and the older people, meanwhile, say three Paternosters. Then Adam Birnmoser announces the next items on the agenda: the Forum, the Palatine, and the Capitol.

"A little paganism after so many churches is like a cup of Turkish coffee after an ordination dinner," Eve declared to her brother as she rushed to breathe the air of classicism and wear out her high heels on these historic stones. There the conspirators stabbed to death the great Julius Caesar! Here Marcus Tullius Cicero forged his golden Latin! There lived the Vestal Virgins, guardians of the sacred fire!

"The bestial virgins?" inquired the sacristan. "That would have been the right school for my old woman."

There the grave of Romulus, here the pillar of Phocas, somewhere else the temple of Esculapius, the Arch of Titus—names and figures flapped round the pilgrims' ears like wet dishcloths, and it was scarcely surprising that, having panted up a hill covered with ruins, they no longer knew if it was the Palatine, the Esquiline, the Aventine or the Zugspitze. And enthusiastically as Birnmoser might point out to them the dead splendor of the Roman empire and the living beauty of domes and towers, it did not rid the impoverished baron of the painful trembling in his knees, nor slake the hop-farmer's measureless thirst; the parish youth group members of both sexes were shaken by periodic fits of yawning; Father Süss kept on groaning that this day was proving more strenuous even than the day of his ordination, and even his athletic sister was so limp that she gratefully accepted Birnmoser's helping arm. Not even the terrifying hole of the Mamertine prison could revive the drooping blossoms of their enthusiasm. Even the schoolmistress's throat was parched; she could only force out a few faint "Ohs" and "Ahs," but she did summon up a final burst of energy on seeing Rome's age-old symbol, the she-wolf, crawling all about with drooling tongue, which drew from Frau Raibeisen, honorary president of her local society for the protection of animals, an enraged cry of "Scandalous!"

Scandalous it also was when, after visiting another two churches, the pilgrims finally sat down to supper in their lodgings and nothing but huge plates of spaghetti

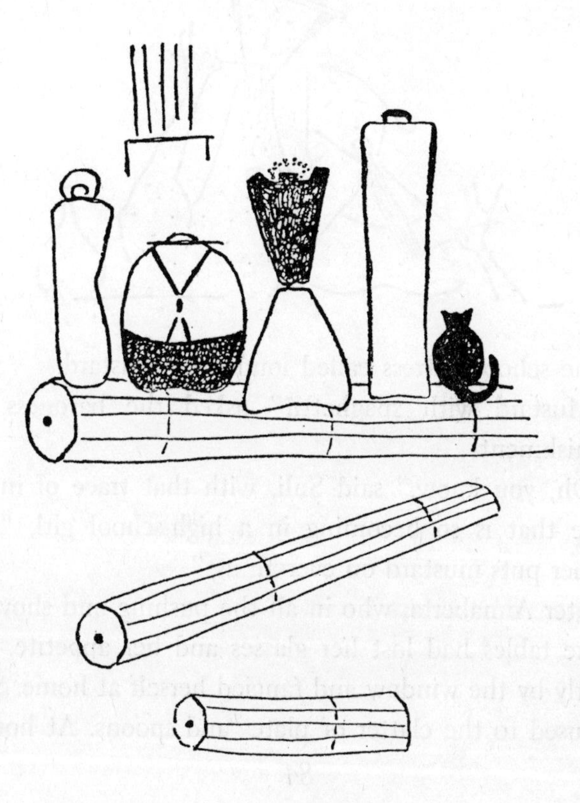

made an appearance. As the wine was not served until half an hour later, our pilgrims, exhausted with heat and admiration, had to expend their last ounce of energy stuffing the spaghetti as best they could into their mouths.

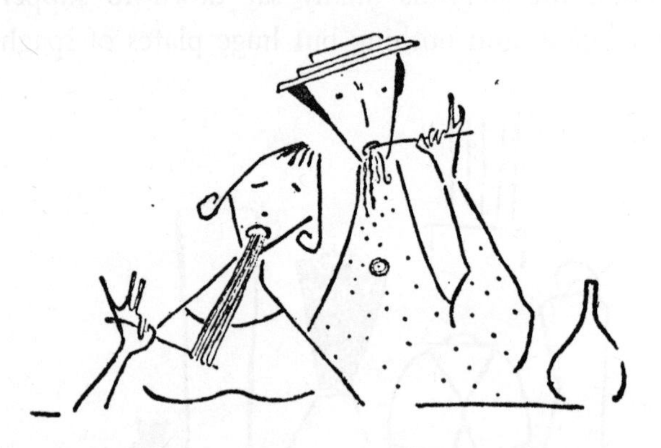

The schoolmistress called loudly for mustard.

"Mustard with spaghetti?" asked the baroness in astonishment.

"Oh, you know," said Suli, with that trace of innocence that is so becoming in a high-school girl, "my mother puts mustard on everything."

Sister Annaberta, who in all the pushing and shoving at the tables had lost her glasses and her appetite, sat quietly by the window and fancied herself at home. She was used to the clatter of plates and spoons. At home, though, the diners' voices had a more contented ring than these here in Rome.

"Tomorrow will not be so strenuous," was Monsignor Schwiefele's final promise before he spoke a short grace and wished them all good night. The pilgrims crept painfully to their rooms and plumped like sacks of flour on their beds. Sister Annaberta opened her window as wide as it would go. A delicious, cool breeze blew in, caressing her cheek like the grateful kisses of her smallest orphans. And suddenly—for this is the land of miracles—the pines and fir-trees from the Bavarian forest came marching along the Via Flaminia, covered the Milvio Bridge, crowded over all the seven hills, and their rustling transformed solemn old Rome into a joyful orphanage. Pope, cardinals, carabinieri, all turned to apple-cheeked toddlers in white, red, and colored smocks, jubilantly throwing tiara, miters, and helmets like rubber balls into the air, swarming all over the marble columns, playing hide and seek in the catacombs and plucking at the sister's habit, cheerfully imploring: "Annaberta! Annaberta!"

5. *Concerning marble hands and golden sands, or why Sister Annaberta first wished her orphan children were with her, and then did not*

The less strenuous day dawned at the stroke of six. The male members of the parish youth group went at the double from door to door, banging everyone awake. While the baroness scrubbed down her husband's bent back with cold water, and Sulamith fretfully declared to her mother that it was "flipping awful" to be turned out of bed so early in the Eternal City—("Shame on you, child, where did you pick up that common expression?" wailed the schoolmistress)—while the monsignor was saying his Lauds in his shirt-sleeves and the chaplain was doing his yoga exercises on the balcony, Luitpold the sacristan and Sister Annaberta were sitting in the lobby, all ready to leave.

"Do you like Rome?" asked the sister, turning to Luitpold.

"What do you think? Cost me a hundred marks."

"And what about our companions?"

"One of 'em, that girl Eve, she's all right. But when you're already hitched—" he heaved a sigh like a brimming bucket from some dank cistern—"and to a dragon like I've got, then—" he sighed again—"then it's better not to think about it."

"But that would be death to your soul, anyway."

"Really?" The sacristan looked up, incredulous. "Do you know what death to the soul is? When your old woman starts hollering at you the minute you get up, and then the priest moans at you in the sacristy because there's a bit of cork in the altar wine. If only I wasn't so patient. But that's just what makes my old woman and the priest so wild."

"You must bear your cross like every good Christian," the sister consoled him.

"What else can I do?" Resigned, he looked down at the floor; then he suddenly rubbed his hands in malicious glee. "But I'm glad the priest will have to manage on his own the day after tomorrow, the holy day of obligation. I'd like to see his face when he can't find the key to the safe where he keeps the special chalice. Because I've got it in my pocket. I suppose he'll blame the servers."

"Those poor creatures will have to take the consequences, you cruel man."

"Me, cruel? And what if he does sling a few of 'em at the wall? That lot grow up far too quickly for our liking," answered Luitpold, adamant, pulling out a vast handkerchief with a view of the city printed on it and complacently blowing his nose right into the Pantheon.

The other pilgrims had meanwhile won their battle with the bedclothes, and were appearing one by one in the lobby. Monsignor Schwiefele's flock, many a lamb only half washed, many a kid unshaven, were presently all assembled. With great satisfaction, a little blood on his chin, and soap behind his ear, the monsignor mustered his charges, clapped his hands, at which the porter, who had dozed off, shot out of his lodge, and announced as number one on the program:

"Communal Mass in Santa Croce di Gerusalemme."

"Jerusalemmer—what kind of a new saint is he?" came in Low German from the most intelligent boy among the Rhinelanders.

"Hey, you're all so Catholic in Bavaria, *you* ought to know." And he tapped the hop-farmer on the shoulder. The latter turned round, swaying his head like a quart pot, and said:

"The Jerusalemmers are an order in which a clod like yourself would get on very well," and turned his back once more.

The Reverend Harald Schlüter celebrated the communal Mass. This was followed by a visit to the church's precious relics, supposed to be unique in the whole world. On hearing the word "relics," Sister Annaberta took refuge among the parish youth group, so as not to let Eve the rationalist shatter the emotions she necessarily felt. It was of little avail. A worm had eaten its way into the juicy apple of her faith, and to cut it out she would have to wait for her confessor's knife.

As far as sights were concerned that morning, they were limiting themselves to one, which, however, contained many hundreds of sights in itself: the Vatican Museum. The less cultured members of the party inquired at breakfast of the schoolmistress and similar oracles what treasures they now had in store. Sonorous names such as Raphael, Fra Angelico, Belvedere, Michelangelo and Laocoön mingled with the clatter of the aluminum cups. Even Annaberta grew quite exalted. It is always the same: a simple soul needs only a sip of the sweet wine of culture to be intoxicated on the spot.

Masses of people were wedged in front of the museum doors. A group of working-class youngsters from Belgium, a Styrian brass band, the Gustavus Adolfus choir of Stockholm, white-clad Japanese women, advocates of female emancipation from Denver, Colorado—indeed representatives from all over the globe were pushing, panting, wincing, cursing and groaning their way through the narrow entrance. Sister Annaberta sailed tactically in the baroness's wake, and thus managed to get towed through the turnstile in one piece. But ever since the time of Hesiod, the gods have made effort precede success, and a spiral staircase had to be climbed before the treasure chests of beauty were revealed.

"Keep together! Everyone keep together!" bellowed the monsignor. Sister Annaberta would not have dreamed of doing otherwise. But suddenly there stood before her, in the shape of Eve Süss, the serpent of Eden as though freshly darting from its tree, and seductively whispering:

"Come with me, Sister. Let's get out of this crush. Herr Birnmoser told me a way we can look at the Sistine in peace. My brother is coming too. Come along." And before the sister could object, Eve had grabbed her sleeve and drawn her into a gallery of maps where the monsignor could not see them. Young Father Alois Süss obediently followed.

Amazement curtailed the custodians' anticlerical jokes when the three lone visitors appeared, breathless as Marathon runners, in the Sistine Chapel.

"We have half an hour before the crowd of tourists gets here," said Eve.

"Herr Birnmoser—what a connoisseur that man is! —advised me to look at the frescoes on the side walls first, and at Michelangelo's ceiling afterwards."

Sister Annaberta took her own cue from this, and conscientiously studied the frescoes by the old masters, finding each one more beautiful than the last. When Eve said: "Now look up," and Annaberta looked up, she clapped her hands with delight. She knew these pictures! They were all familiar to her from reproductions and ordination cards. Only, here they were a thousand times more beautiful. Especially the one where God the Father is touching Adam with his finger and Adam is waking to life. If the sister could have had her way, she would have lain down flat on her back to gaze her fill at the face of the Creator, the heavenly beauty of the first man and woman, the prophets' fathomless gravity, and the ravishing mien of the sibyls—but the custodians forbade it.

"We'd better not look too closely at the Last Judgment on the altar wall. For one thing, it has been spoilt by restorers, and for another, it upsets the harmony of the room," said Eve Süss. What a talented girl she was!

"The children of this world are always cleverer than

the children of light, aren't they, Father?" said Annaberta to the young priest, catching him in the act of yawning and forgetting to put his hand over his mouth.

As the narrow doorway then disgorged the first gaggle of Swiss high-school girls, breathing heavily with wonderment, our three lone rangers took to their heels and fought through to a second chapel; the chapel of Nicolas V, where the painter-monk of Fiesole has charmed onto the walls the legends of the deacons Stephen and Lawrence. Not one of the three uttered a word. The glorious

paintings spoke all the more effectively in the dusky room. "Oh, if only my orphans were here," thought Annaberta, "they would understand these pictures too. How beautifully I could tell them the story of the first martyr Stephen."

Annaberta had up to now been all in favor of what she had been shown. But now, hurrying along corridors lined with drunken satyrs, battered graces, snub-nosed philosophers, bald-headed caesars and broken gods, all in naked marble, she regretted having paid her entrance money. Good heavens, into what a jungle of immodesty had the monsignor led her? Did all that really belong to the Holy Father? Hard to believe. But perhaps he knows as little about their existence as he does of those irregularities to which Reverend Father Schlüter intends to draw his attention?

Eve Süss seemed not to share such scruples. "Aren't these figures marvellous, Sister? Just look at this bust of Antinous, what classical symmetry! He was the Emperor Hadrian's favorite, you know. Or here, the delicate proportions of this impudent bacchante."

Bust, favorite, bacchante—brrr, all that smacked of a world Annaberta wanted absolutely nothing to do with.

"Yes, it's beautiful," she sighed, "but all the same, I'm glad now my orphans had to stay at home."

Father Süss, whose attempts at speech today had mostly collapsed into fits of yawning, turned to her and said:

"Children are only let in when it isn't washing-day. Tomorrow these emperors and gods will all have clean clothes on again."

"Alois, don't be so silly," Eve reprimanded him, and turning affectionately to Annaberta, she added: "I can understand your feelings. Thousands of other people must feel the same way. But tell me honestly: is not the human body as God created it a lovely and noble thing?"

"Of course," Annaberta nodded, "as God created it. But I think that what people turn it into doesn't always correspond with the Creator's intention." Eve was silent, and having walked pensively on for a few yards, she regretted that the sister did not even come up to her shoulder; for she would so much have liked to be able to look up to her.

They suddenly came upon the schoolmistress plus daughter. These too had branched off on their own, and were just peering intently at a marble figure lacking what every Prussian soldier, even in the highest ranks, must have, and which, anyway, is considered of vital importance: a head. It was the torso of the Belvedere. Before it stood the schoolmistress. She had put on her best glasses and was examining the famous work from all angles, her sharp nose almost scraping the marble. Then she took two steps backwards, folded her hands over her stomach, and said, loud enough for all to hear:

"You must change your ways."

"What again, Mummy?" asked Sulamith.

The schoolmistress clicked her tongue with annoyance.

"Stupid girl, can't you see that I am merely quoting what Rainer Maria——"

"Ah, the prince of Monaco."

"Idiot! Rainer Maria Rilke!—what he felt on looking at this torso, and he was quite right."

Our deserters finally came upon the monsignor in the Cortile del Belvedere, where he was expertly analyzing what had been wrongly added to the Laocoön group. Sister Annaberta would have liked to slip back unnoticed into the crowd, but her white wimple could not escape his reverence's piercing spectacles. He frowned most ungraciously:

"You vowed obedience, my dear Sister. That is the second time you have taken the law into your own hands. The third time, I shall have to inform your mother superior."

Docile as a whipped dog, Annaberta shuffled along in the wake of the crowd of pilgrims. Once more she found herself in the chapel of Nicolas V, once more in the Sistine Chapel. This last was now a confused babble of voices, like a debate on beer prices in the Bavarian legislative assembly. She listened to no explanatory words, nor did she strain her eyes any further. She kept to one side the whole time, murmuring one Ave after another for the battered graces, the snub-nosed philosophers, for the emperors and their favorites, whose bodies could be gaped at by all and sundry, but whose poor souls, however, even the monsignor had probably forgotten.

*

When they came out at last onto an open terrace, they thought that perhaps that was the end of their ration of culture for one day; but no, they were once more herded on, into a large reddish building, the "Pinacoteca." The parish youth group of both sexes would have liked to take this hurdle, the last between them and their eagerly awaited lunch, at a gallop. That, however, was not allowed. Firstly, they were in a city whose great age kept the working tempo of its inhabitants within reasonable bounds; and secondly they belonged to a nation of thinkers and poets, a title that imposes an obligation all the greater for being no longer valid.

And so, like wrynecks, our dear pilgrims twisted their heads to and fro in the Quattrocento and Cinquecento, delighted, in passing, at Melozzo da Forli's cherubs, fought their way through to the Raphael room, lingered dutifully in front of the famous tapestries, fumbled for suitable adjectives, and then swept on past the Seicento and the Settecento towards the fresh air. Now at last they were allowed to peep into the gardens of the Vatican, revelling in lush greens after so much oil-paint and marble.

Miss Emerenz Obermair sighed: "Oh, if only the Holy Father would come out for a walk, just for a few minutes."

"But that wouldn't get you an indulgence, Miss," the sacristan interrupted her roughly, for he hated female devotees as much as he hated bailiffs. Emerenz made no reply, but puckered up her mouth so that the hairs on her upper lip quivered in the breath from her nostrils, and looked at him with contempt, as if to say: "And what do *you* know about holy theology?"

When the monsignor had collected his flock around him he asked what they had liked most. Simmerl, the hop-farmer, chose the pine-cone decorations, Baron von Neuhaus the porphyry sarcophagus of Helena. A few Rhenish youths hesitated between the indirect lighting in the chapel of Nicolas V and Apollo slaying the dragon. The girls wiped their lips as though they had been licking ice-cream, and breathed "Raphael." The newly ordained priest, himself as lean as Leonardo's Saint Jerome, said he had been most impressed by the fat paunches that the baroque painters had put on all their male figures, even though in the seventeenth century there were no corporation officials they could have used as models.

They had another hour before lunch. What should they do? Eve proposed that having studied the painters' colors they should now study those of the Creator by sitting in the sun and contemplating the Roman sky, but her suggestion found little approval with those people who regarded a holiday as hard labor. In order to avoid a democratic discussion prolonged *ad infinitum*, all were unanimous in invoking the spirit of clericalism, and the final decision was left to the priests. After a brief debate, Monsignor Schwiefele and Chaplain Schlüter decided on the Capuchin crypt in the Viale

Vittorio Veneto, no doubt so as to counter the intoxicating array of pagan beauty with a powerfully baroque *memento mori*.

On hearing the words "Capuchin crypt," the baroness and the baron shed a furtive tear (they were such a happily married couple really!), for both were thinking of the Capuchin crypt in Vienna, last resting-place of the revered imperial house. This time, of course, they were not to see archdukes in pewter, but the bones of Franciscan monks. Annaberta was not quite clear whether it was four or forty thousand Capuchins whose skulls, instead of being allowed to turn peacefully to dust, had to provide a thrill of pious horror for schoolchildren from the Campagna and Irish parliamentarians. The number, in any case, was unimportant. She held her breath in awe. The empty eye-sockets seemed to be staring straight at her, the skeletons pointing their scourges—might these holding the scourges have been priors?—at her alone. On hearing that the bones had also been used as stucco in the chapel, she did not find the idea lacking in taste, as did the Reverend Harald Schlüter, but weird enough all the same. They were, after all, the bones of holy men! "If we at home," she thought, "were instructed to plaster our walls with the bones of our holy sisters, our chapel would be as solemn as a waiting-room."

A painful incident then took place.

At the entry to the grottoes sat a very young, downy-bearded priest, delicate as spring spinach, who, with unceasing murmurs of "Grazie," was receiving alms. He had up to now looked indifferently through the pilgrims, but he suddenly jumped up, crying, "Stop, stop!" and charged through to the farthest grotto, where Emerenz Obermair—she is attracting a lot of attention today—was just in the act of smuggling a small Capuchin collarbone into the capacious bag where she carried all her aids to devotion. "Stop, stop!" he called again, seizing

her so expertly by the collar that he might have spent his novitiate at Scotland Yard. But Emerenz's conscience was thickly padded, and she explained quite calmly

that she had not dreamed of stealing the bone, she merely wanted to take away a little souvenir of this holy place. What did one collarbone more or less matter anyway? She would have it put in a silver setting when she got home, and give it pride of place in her reliquary. She was, moreover, quite willing to present the monastery in exchange with a gallstone taken from the Regensburg clergyman for whom she had once worked. The young Capuchin, who did not understand a word, kept countering her bombardments with energetic cries of: "To the guardian! To the guardian!" At last Emerenz was forced to follow him out. Her fellow pilgrims stood watching the incident, some amused, others angry, but all of them helpless.

Emerenz appeared at the monastery door ten minutes later triumphantly waving the collarbone she had fought for and won. She told them that the guardian had first mumbled Latin in his beard, then let loose a broadside of Italian. When she had informed him of her German nationality by making signs (whatever might they have been?), his eyes had begun to sparkle, and he had thrice enthusiastically pronounced the name "Adenauer." For love of Adenauer he had made her a present of the collarbone, but to show her gratitude, she had pressed a banknote into his hand, telling him to spend it on getting his church thoroughly dusted for once. He had looked rather sour at this, but had then nodded and dismissed her with a blessing.

"All right, then," the monsignor closed Emerenz's report. He was glad that no worse vexation had arisen. "And now lunch." Lunch was rice soup, tuna fish and chocolate pudding. So that they could properly digest not only this delicate mixture, but also the Jove of Otricoli and the Aldobrandini Nuptials, Birnmoser ordered all the pilgrims to bed. The short siesta worked wonders. Soon after two o'clock they clambered into their coaches, fresh and ready for anything. Out they went, past the site of the World Exhibition and into the Campagna. The parish youth group members whistled "Beyond gray city walls," Sulamith read from Goethe's *Journey to Italy*, and Sister Annaberta had live cell therapy explained to her by the medical student.

The air was suddenly rent by a cry that made the drivers jam on their brakes, thinking someone had been killed. It was only that the landlubbers had spied the sea. All, with the exception of the schoolmistress, who from her journeys to England was as familiar with the Channel as was her daughter with the *Études* of Clementi, craned their necks to look out of the windows, even short-sighted Sister Annaberta. The sea, the sea! Then they were as suddenly silent, talking only in whispers. Such a fit of the doldrums did not suit the chaplain. He encouraged his youth club to start up a sea shanty. They knew none. "Schleswig-Holstein, sea-girt land" was familiar only to the more mature members. "Then any other song dealing with water. . . ." Again the youngsters pondered, and then, to the softly purring accompaniment of the engines, a piano porter and a hairdresser from Kohlenpott struck up in perfect harmony with a folk song: "I go to the well, but will not drink," and sang so affectingly that when they got to the line about the "Darling of my heart," even the highly intellectual Sulamith had to apply to her mother for the loan of a handkerchief.

In Nettuno the monsignor divided his people into sexes and three ranks, and led them in an orderly procession to the church of Saint Maria Goretti. Everyone said a few prayers of their own, and then he gave a short sermon on the words of the Saviour: "The light of thy body is thy eye. If thy eye be single, thy whole body will be lightsome," begging the young people in particular to keep a pure heart and a clear mind at a time that is rapidly going out of joint. After the loud amen—which for many came too soon, so affected they were by his plain, heartfelt words—after the amen the monsignor made a particularly happy announcement.

"Tomorrow morning at ten o'clock we are going to have a special audience with the Pope."

It was just as well they were in church. The pilgrims

might have knocked the good monsignor down in their joy. When they got outside, everyone demanded details, but he only grinned and said nothing.

And now they had two hours before their return. Everyone had carte blanche: they could go for a bathe, visit the American military cemetery, stroll through Nettuno or indulge in a little *dolce far niente.*

The male representatives of the parish youth group decided on a swim.

"You too, Chaplain?" asked Monsignor Schwiefele.

"Why not? God's Church needs healthy bodies as well as clever heads."

"Of course, of course. And yet I wouldn't appear in front of the faithful in a bathing-costume."

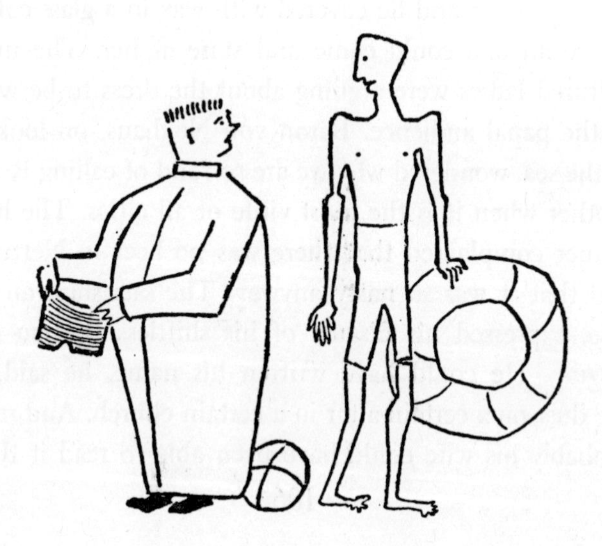

"That is quite understandable, Monsignor," replied the chaplain, patting in almost friendly fashion on the monsignor's stomach. Everyone laughed, the monsignor loudest of all. "In any case, we shall go into the water so far away from the town that not even the school-mistress with her telescope will be able to see us."

And off they went, to grapple with sharks and get stung by sea-urchins, while the non-swimmers refreshed themselves in a nearby restaurant, buying up nearly its whole supply of lemonade and keeping the jukebox going. Emerenz Obermair, that walking information bureau and specialist in indulgences, wrote to her friend Kreszenz Schwammweiser that it was very nice in Nettuno, but that she would not like to be the holy virgin Maria Goretti and lie covered with wax in a glass coffin, where anyone could come and stare at her. The more cultured ladies were arguing about the dress to be worn at the papal audience. Baron von Neuhaus, on looking at the sea, wondered why we are so fond of calling Rome mother when it is the most virile of all cities. The hop-farmer complained that there was no beer in Nettuno, and that it was so nasty anyway. The sacristan, on his side, expressed his disgust of his shiftless Roman colleagues. He could have written his name, he said, in the dust on a certain altar in a certain church. And most probably his wife could have been able to read it there when she came to Rome next year with the Friends of Saint Rita.

Sister Annaberta was not in the restaurant. Eve had gone with her to the beach and had helped her up onto a jutting rock. She stared entranced at the sea, feeling she could look at it for ever. At her feet it was dark blue, like the Madonna's mantle. Then it paled towards the horizon, sailing boats gliding over its surface like angels bringing joyful news from heaven. Annaberta's poor eyesight could not make out the line between sea and sky. And thus, for her, the two melted into one gleaming azure bell, and she was the clapper, blissfully proclaiming the feast of God's infinite generosity.

Sister Annaberta closed her eyes, the better to lock all this splendor, all this happiness deep in the treasure-chest of her heart. Then she became all the more aware of the breath of the sea, the rhythm of that pilgrimage creation has been making for millions of years. She knew by heart the chorale of the pine forests, and the full orchestra of the thunderstorms, the billowing pulse of the cornfields when the wind caresses each delicate stalk—and now it was vouchsafed to her to know the sea, God's oldest friend. Even before the Creator said: "Let there be light," it was there, and His spirit moved upon it. The nun's heart fluttered with sheer gratitude like a young bird, fallen from its nest, that struggles to reach a helping branch. "If only my orphans were here, if only my orphans were here," she whispered again and again, because it is hard, even for a nun who has said farewell to the world, to bear so much happiness alone.

She shook herself suddenly and turned to Eve:

"I wish I could swim."

"I wish I could write" was the student's reply.

"Write? Why?"

"A gift for poetry and as much free time as the president of a legislative assembly! Then I'd write an account of our journey as different from all those grave, erudite books on Rome as *Der Rosenkavalier* is from *Tristan und Isolde*. And whereas I should only touch on the obvious, official aspect of such a journey, I should paint in loving detail all the private and personal impressions, and more than anything I should emphasize the comic element. Ironical, irenical. Maybe a lot of people would turn up their noses—the wine of Cana is not enough for many Christians. But if we lose the power to laugh at ourselves, haven't our enemies every cause to make us weep?" Sister Annaberta nodded in amazement; Eve really was an extraordinary girl.

The student pointed across to the restaurant: "You only have to consider the priceless characters in our mixed bag of pilgrims. The monsignor, with sweat pouring from his brow and even more goodness pouring from his soul. Frau Raibeisen the schoolmistress and her daughter—I feel sure they were born with spectacles over their eyes, were weaned on Knigge's *Book of Etiquette,* and rocked to sleep with Schiller's *Song of the Bell.* And then that man Birnmoser, who really makes me quite cross sometimes."

At that moment, thank goodness, a ship's siren wailed, otherwise at her next confession Eve would have had a lot to admit in connection with the ninth commandment.

The two free hours soon passed. The pilgrims returned to Rome via Castel Gandolfo, paid a quick visit to the Pantheon, and ended the day with devotions in Santa Maria Maggiore. Tomorrow they were to stand face to face with the Holy Father! This thought gave many a nervous soul the jitters, and Birnmoser had to dispense several liters of wine to make sure that everyone felt suitably drowsy, and that no one would appear before the Vicar of Christ with bags under their eyes. Before we send our pilgrims to the Vatican tomorrow morning, however—the chaplain with his memorandum concerning the irregularities in the Church, the baron in a stiffly creased suit, the nun with a pounding heart, Sulamith got up like a Miss Universe on her sixtieth birthday—let us be indiscreet and take a look at the letter which the schoolmistress wrote to her spouse Cornelius on the eve of that happy day.

"Beloved husband," the words rippled from her pen. "Such then are my greetings from the Eternal City. I will not contend that either it or the journey gains my unqualified approval, but thanks to the fact that, remembering Professor Wirrig's recommendations, I made a most intensive study of the history of *Roma aeterna* before undertaking this trip, I can grade the results up to now as good to satisfactory. Our companions correspond more to the price level of the trip than to what I should have liked, but no censure is expressed, or even implied, in this. (Has the gas-man been? I left the correct amount of money in the third drawer on the left.) A person of our class and rank must perforce submit to a certain isolation. Suli is in every respect what I hoped for from a daughter of yours. She stays faithfully by my side, refusing to be influenced, even less to be impressed, by certain more lax conceptions prevalent here by the Méditerranée—my use of the French word is deliberate. We were at the sea today. The young people thought only of bathing, I of Debussy. I hope you are well. You must be grateful that I schooled you in domestic tasks at an early stage. It saves us having to have a woman in. I close, dearest husband, with a few lines from Goethe, written while he was in

Rome: 'But what is greatest of all, and what I never felt e'er now: whoever has eyes to see and looks about him in an earnest spirit, *must* grow worthy.' Ever your own Alwine."

6. *Concerning the cat-catcher of Trastevere, or how the reverend sister came to a child*

How wonderful the audience with the Pope had been! They had all knelt down before him, before the Holy Father of Christendom, had respectfully kissed his ring and listened with joy to the words he had addressed to each person in his own language. At last—they had not noticed the passage of time—he had invited them all with one of those deliberate, insistent gestures that are made only by men of solitary greatness, to group themselves around him for a photograph. They were all to have a souvenir of this longed-for moment. Finally they had knelt down once more to receive his blessing. The Holy Father had disappeared into his apartments again by the time Annaberta raised her eyes from the floor. How wonderful it had been—apart from a small contretemps for which Sister Annaberta will reproach herself (though not, of course, so very much) all the rest of her days. But what contretemps?

Well, it was the Holy Father's practice to make a small sign of the cross over anything in bags or boxes that people cared to offer for his blessing. Happy but confused, Sister Annaberta had opened her own bag, but at the wrong compartment, and thus the Holy Father had made a solemn, dignified sign of the cross not over rosaries and medallions, but over a pink marzipan pig, donkeys that could run down a sloping surface, dolls

that rolled their eyes, cloth monkeys, a wax elephant printed with the words *Anno Santo*, several Saint Peter's churches made of chocolate, some dainty little cardinal's hats, and all the other edible and inedible toys that Sister Annaberta had bought for her orphan children. She was horribly embarrassed, all the more so because the Holy Father had not even noticed her blunder. The schoolmistress had, you may be sure, and naturally she reported it to the other ladies the moment the audience was over, at which Sister Annaberta could have sunk through the marble floor with shame. Be that as it may, what happened was that she crept out of the Vatican hanging her head so low that she lost sight of her travelling companions. And now she stood all alone in Saint Peter's Square, with not a word of Italian except "Santo Padre" and "Mille grazie."

Surely they had turned left to come into the square? Sister Annaberta therefore had to keep to the right if she wanted to go back the way they had come. She got mixed up inadvertently with a swarm of American matrons listening, delighted but tired, to their guide. "They are sure to be heading for the station," murmured Annaberta, deciding to swim with this tide of democratic American daughters. She could get from the station on her own. But, oh dear, at the very next open square the ladies climbed into an azure-blue coach and roared off to the next item on their schedule.

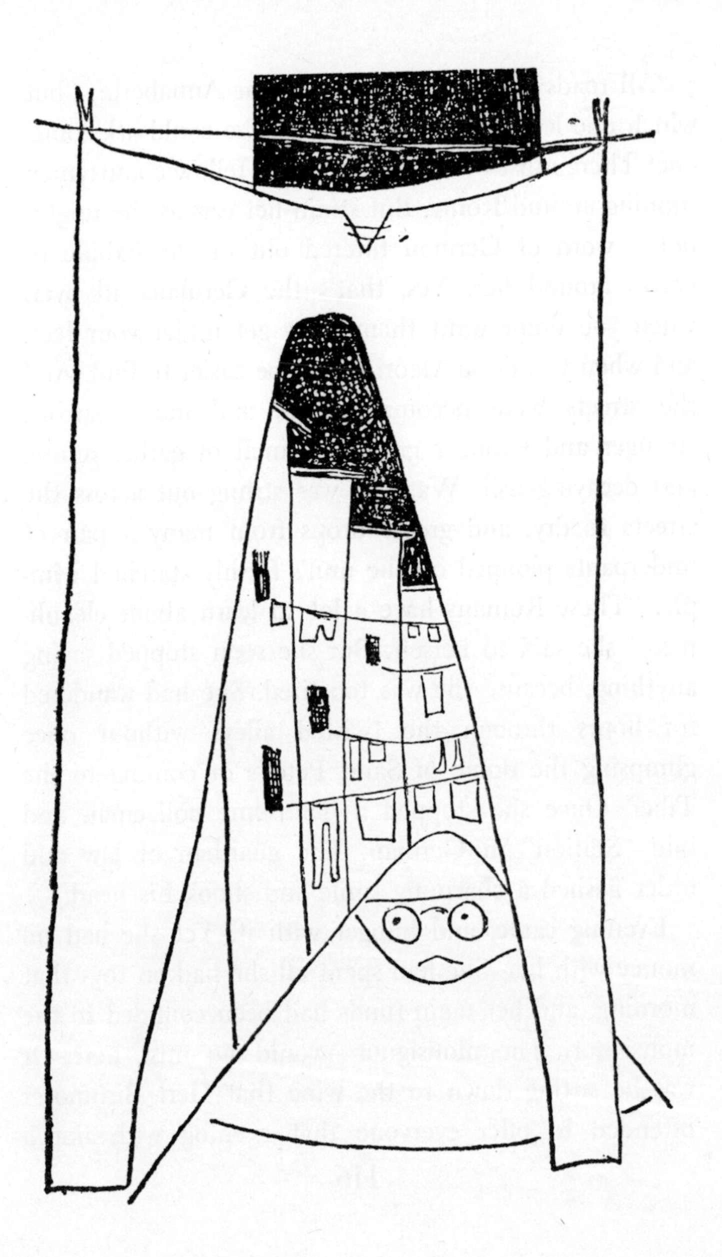

"All roads lead to Rome," thought Annaberta, "but which one leads out of it?" If only she could ask someone! There must be thousands of her fellow countrymen running around Rome. But strain her ears as she might, not a word of German filtered out of the babble of voices around her. Yes, that's the Germans all over, when you don't want them, they get under your feet, and when you do, a Maori would be easier to find. And the streets were becoming more and more narrow, stronger and stronger grew the smell of garlic, refuse, and decaying fish. Washing was strung out across the streets to dry, and greasy drops from many a pair of underpants plopped on the nun's freshly starched wimple. "These Romans have a lot to learn about cleanliness," she said to herself. But she soon stopped saying anything, because she was too tired. She had wandered for hours through the twisted alleys without once glimpsing the dome of Saint Peter's or coming to the Tiber. Once she stopped a handsome policeman and said "Station" in German. The guardian of law and order flashed a charming smile and shook his head.

Evening came, and hunger with it. Yet she had no money with her. She had spent all she had on toys that morning, and her main funds had been confided to the monsignor. The monsignor—would he miss her? Or was he sitting down to the wine that Herr Birnmoser intended to offer everyone that evening with not a thought for the poor nun blistering her feet on the pavements of Trastevere?

Benches are unknown in this part of Rome, so she sank down exhausted on a doorstep. She tried to pacify her rumbling stomach. But once roused, brother body is not to be gainsaid, and at last Annaberta, sick at heart, bit off the head of the marzipan pig that had been blessed by the Pope.

Brother body, however, did not cease his complaints until he had engulfed the whole pig, and a chocolate Saint Peter's as well. And now the stars were shining above Rome. Sister Annaberta saw nothing of them, for she had long since dozed off in the doorway of that old house in Trastevere. Bells tinkled from countless churches and chapels; she started now and then at the far-off clanging of a street car, or a drunken curse uttered by a descendant of the holy martyrs. Was it already past midnight when hunger woke her? She did not know. A cool wind idled through the streets. Somewhere a fiddle scraped, and a floorboard creaked under a heavy tread. Never before had the sister been in a city of two million people, and never before had she been so alone. And that was why she wept.

All at once, something sprang into her lap: something warm and alive, that burrowed, seeking protection, into the folds of her skirt. A little cat.

Heartened by the creature's trustful action, Annaberta was about to stroke its soft fur and take its little paws in her hand when the harsh light of a torch suddenly fell upon her, and a voice shouted angry words that no doubt meant: "Hand over that cat!" So, at all events, did the cat interpret them, for it mewed pitiably, snuggling deeper into the voluminous folds of her habit.

"Leave the cat alone," Annaberta said firmly to the dark figure.

"Ma chè, German?" came the amazed response.

"Yes, thank God—you too?" Sister Annaberta jumped up joyfully, whereupon the cat dropped to the ground and fled.

"No, no," said the man. "I was many years work in

Germania. I hate all Germans, I like kill them, like the cat. Where is cat? Give me, you!"

"The cat has run away, look for it yourself."

"And what we eat tomorrow? Tomorrow festo. And I have ten little children, very hungry. S-o-o-o hungry." The man drummed with both fists on his stomach, to demonstrate all the more insistently to the nun the agonizing need of his offspring, whom she had deprived of their festive dinner. Annaberta ought actually at this point to have asked the way to the station, but the thought of ten starving children stifled any worry about her own plight.

"Take me to your children," she resolutely commanded. As with a priest who is dragged from sleep to hurry to the bedside of a dying person, all her weariness had gone.

On realizing that she meant what she said, the man admitted in a small voice that five of the children had already died—from starvation, of course. Annaberta's honest mind could still not see through this good-for-nothing. She clasped her head in her hands, loudly lamenting so much hardship. The man saw she was not very steady on her feet, offered her his arm, and introduced himself as "Gino, the cat-catcher." At the third lamp-post he informed her that of his five living children, three were for the time being with relatives in the country, and so the sister would only find two. "All the better," thought Annaberta, "there wouldn't have been enough in my bag for five."

The cat-catcher said at last: "Careful, my house," and pushed the nun into a dank, gloomy passage. Fear crawled over her. How could she have been so senseless as to follow this criminal? Who could tell what he wanted of her? Perhaps he was mad enough to think she was carrying a lot of money, and intended to stick a knife into her back; or to strangle her like a cat, and bury her somewhere outside the city gates——?

But things had not yet come to such a pass: they then entered a vaulted room with a floor of beaten earth, walls sparsely whitewashed, and a narrow, barred window that served as a chimney, the only window in this "dwelling." Thus, then, lived the outcasts in the Eternal City!

The light from the torch slid over the floor and finally picked out a boy of five or six, curled up like a hedgehog, who lay snoring on a pile of old cat-skins. "Palmiro," explained Gino.

"And where is the other child?" asked Annaberta, vexed that of ten supposed victims of starvation, only one remained.

Gino shook Palmiro till he awoke, and shouted something in his ear about a bambina. The child blinked, terrified, in the harsh light, waved towards a corner of the room behind him, and rolled himself up again to sleep.

"Palmiro say bambina in the corner," said Gino.

"Which corner?"

"We must look, will find," came the resigned answer.

Sister Annaberta was on the brink of flying into a rage, but she remembered in time a saying of her reverend mother's, that one must wrap poor sinners not in the brown paper of anger, but in the cotton wool of Christian kindness. Only for a short while, however, did she manage to soothe her over-agitated nerves. When she finally unearthed a baby of about six months in the darkest corner, peeled off its rags and held the little body up to the light—Oh, God, she had never seen a child so filthy, so thin—her patience was shattered and she cried:

"What inhuman creature has this child got for a mother? Where is she, what's she up to at this hour of the night? Bring her to me, and I'll slap her face till she learns a few lessons in child care. Go on, fetch her here!"

Gino said despondently: "She is in America, Suora."

"In America? What's she doing in America?"

"She no tell me. She go away in the middle of the night, with Giacomo."

"Who is Giacomo?" she inquired, whereupon Gino

roared a terrifying curse and shook his fist towards heaven. Annaberta understood.

"This child is going to die. Her little heart is only just beating."

Gino sat down on an upturned bucket, thrust his knife into the floor, and said in a quiet voice:

"Why bambina must live? If she die, she know nothing, feel nothing. No more trouble. Why she must live? In Trastevere life no good. If police take me away —who feed bambina? Palmiro old enough, Palmiro find food, drink. But no bambina. You want bambina be like her mother? No, you no want that. You good. You so good, so good; you no kill cats. But, let bambina die. Let bambina die!" he implored, and when he began to howl, then the tears ran down Annaberta's face too.

At about this hour, in an orphanage on the other side of the Alps, Reverend Mother Potentia awoke from a restless sleep. She had had a nightmare, in which she had seen Annaberta's face, twitching with fear. Mother Potentia got up, lit a candle in front of Our Lady of Succor, said an Ave for her spiritual daughter, and another for the souls in purgatory.

At about this same hour, in a Roman police station, Monsignor Schwiefele was fighting a battle of windmills against the drowsiness of the authorities. They utterly refused to see why they should curtail the well-earned slumbers of their men by combing the city for a stray nun who at daybreak would probably find her own way home.

At about this same hour, Adam Birnmoser and Eve Süss were spooning chocolate ice cream from glass bowls at a gelateria in the Via Nazionale. They were talking —quite impersonally, mark you, for that was Eve the student's favorite level of conversation—about the joys of family life. Still deeply impressed by the audience with the Pope, Birnmoser decided he would give his heir the name of John. Eve Süss looked him firmly in the eye and said pertly that Adam would really be much more suitable. Birnmoser reddened, looked down almost guiltily, and murmured: "Oh, Eve, why do you always see right through me?"

At about the same time too—though here in India the morning was already far advanced—Father Toni—sorry, Father Timotheus, was reading a letter from his mother, as he always secretly thought of Sister Annaberta. She was very close to him at that moment, with her round face, her knowing little eyes entrenched behind thick glasses, her ever-rosy cheeks, the faint moustache on her upper lip, and her many, many wrinkles. She would surely acquire at least three more of these if she ever found out that in the Indian jungle a dry shaver can only be used as a decoration for the wall.

And at the same hour, the light went out behind the second window on the top floor of the Vatican. The Holy Father said his night prayers, commended the whole sleeping world into the hands of its Creator, and with his own right hand made the sign of the cross over Rome.

"Gino," said Sister Annaberta kindly, leaning over him and touching his tousled hair, "don't be upset, Gino. If God calls the bambina, we can't hold her back. But supposing He does call her, do you know if He has a place ready for her in heaven?"

"God does not know the bambina, Suora," answered Gino heavily.

"Haven't you even had her baptized? Hey, answer me!" Gino shook his head. The sister's pity changed straight to righteous indignation: "And you would have let her die unbaptized? A child is not a cat, Gino. A child has an immortal soul, just as you have, don't you forget it. And now get me some water, clean water, go on. Off with you!" She hauled him off the bucket and pushed him to the door. "Dreadful man! No, wait. And remember to get some milk. That's just as important."

"Milk? Where I find milk?" he answered sullenly.

"A scoundrel like yourself should easily be able to find some milk." She got at his professional honor—and it worked. He picked up two bowls and disappeared.

"Conditions like those in ancient Rome," thought the nun. "That's what happens when people don't bother to listen to pastoral letters about family life. Of course the child will die if no one bothers about her. And it may be just as well."

Gino returned with milk and water, which he handed to the sister. Cautiously she tried to coax some milk into the child's mouth. She did not know what to make of the white liquid at first, and dribbled it out again. Then she began to swallow, but so feebly, so listlessly, as though there were no more irksome task in this world than that of keeping alive.

"Now, first a wash, then the baptism. There are more than enough dirty creatures in the Holy Church," said Annaberta, with a reproving glance at Gino. He did not answer; his arms hung slack at his sides, and when the sister removed the coating of dirt from his daughter and held her out to him, he did not even look up. The bambina opened her dark eyes, blinking in amazement at the papa who was unwilling to allow the waters of comfort to trickle over her head, thus granting her an entry into the kingdom of heaven. Since she was about to administer a sacrament, the nun smoothed out her rum-

pled skirt, tweaked her wimple into place, and wiped the sweat from her brow.

"Well, Gino," she said, "I'm ready. What is the baby's name to be?"

"Bambina enough. Why other name? She die anyway."

"One moment, you rascal," thought the sister. "You want your daughter to wander round paradise like some nameless thing? She shall have a name, even if she has no mother and father waiting for her there." She took a little water in the palm of her hand, poised it over the little head, began:

"Bambina——" and hesitated. Was it because she felt so exhausted, or was it the delight of turning a child of man into a child of God that confused her? For she could think of no name but her own. And so she continued: "Annaberta, I baptize you in the name of the Father, the Son, and the Holy Ghost," pouring the water over the child's head. She was flooded with unspeakable joy. To be sure, God had chosen this moment for her to get lost and to run into the cat-catcher! Who, otherwise, would have baptized this little creature? Gino might now do with her what he wanted, she had presented heaven with a new citizen.

Then Gino interrupted her self-consolation.

"And now? To who does belong bambina?"

"To God."

"Not to Pope?"

"To the Pope as well. He is God's representative."

"So, take bambina to the Pope."

"Gino, what are you thinking of?"

"Well—Pope is rich, Pope sleep in bed of purissimo gold, Pope can educate bambina, Pope can keep bambina, give her away, sell, what Pope want."

"What a lot of nonsense. The Pope has no room for a babe in arms."

"So, no room. And live in a big palace, and Gino must live in this little hole. Gino no can feed bambina."

The cat-catcher seemed deadly serious in his intention to get rid of the child.

"So take the bambina to a children's home," suggested Annaberta.

"I no go to police with this—what you call her?"

"Annaberta."

"Who is called Annaberta? Nobody in Trastevere."

"I am called Annaberta," said the sister appeasingly.

"O prima, primissima! Then bambina is your child," he cried, clapping his hands. "Pope will give you much money, you will make bambina to beautiful child. Primissima!"

"What are you thinking of? I can't just——" she stopped. "What can't I?" she asked herself. "Can't I take the child? Does it matter whether I have twenty-two children to look after, or twenty-three?"

"What you can't?" he persisted.

"Throw the child at the feet of the papal guards," she cried in despair, hiding her face in her hands.

"Then the bambina die, bambina Annaberta—" he drawled, strongly emphasizing each syllable of the name so that it rang in the sister's ears like the tolling of a mighty bell. Her hands fell from her face, she bent over the child and slipped the corner of her handkerchief, soaked in milk, between the baby's lips, watching her attempting to slake her thirst.

"So be it, in God's name," she breathed, resolute as an aged bishop who knows that the time has come for him to resign from his chapter, and making a small sign of the cross over the child's breast.

The bambina having drunk her fill, Annaberta's own hunger once more proclaimed itself. She asked Gino if he had anything she could eat.

"Cold cat," was his answer. The sister shuddered.

"Nothing else?"

"Olives. Old cheese. There—" he said, pointing to a tin box.

"Will you please bring me some? I have to hold the child."

He brought her a handful of olives. The old cheese was nibbled all over. Rats, no doubt. Annaberta pushed it aside in disgust.

"Perhaps I'd rather have a piece of cat after all." Gino grinned in triumph.

Surprisingly enough, the meat was well cooked. It tasted rather like the lamb they ate on Easter Day. Only, while eating, she had to try not to think of her beloved Peterle, the orphanage's proudest and loveliest tomcat. But as often happens, there must have been a secret understanding between the cats of Trastevere and the cats of the Bavarian forest, for she had just begun almost to enjoy the tender flesh when, out in the gloomy passage, a tomcat mewed, just as sentimentally, just as longingly, as Peterle. Annaberta's mouthful stuck in her throat. Gino whistled enterprisingly through his teeth, grabbed his knife, and disappeared into the passage.

"Stay here, Gino! Leave the cat alone," the sister implored. In vain. One last, wild miaow—and Gino returned, holding up to the light a plump tomcat with blood dripping from its gashed throat. "Our festo dinner!" he cried in triumph. Annaberta spat her half-chewed mouthful at his feet. Her hunger had gone. So had Gino's pride.

It was not long before sleep overcame both of them. Daylight was oozing through the barred window when Annaberta awoke. She knelt down on the floor to say her prayers. Giggling laughter suddenly roused her from her devotions. Palmiro, wearing only a short little vest, was turning somersaults, so delighted was he by the sight of the sister on her knees. He seemed to think that now his papa would get up and beat her. Why else should she have knelt down?

Annaberta tried to be cross; but in the end she could only join in his laughter. He looked so funny, this cat-catcher's heir from Trastevere, popping up and down on the heap of rags that served him as a bed, showing first his black curly head, then his white backside.

"Palmiro," called the sister enticingly, and when he

crawled nearer, she pulled from her huge bag everything she had bought for the children in the orphanage: the rubber bear, the cloth monkey, the wax elephant printed with the words *Anno Santo*, the donkeys that could run on their own. She arranged all the toys on the floor as lovingly as though she were setting up a Christmas crib.

"They have all been blessed by the Holy Father," she said, thinking: "Even if no priest ever comes into this house, these toy animals will carry God's blessing."

Palmiro gazed and gazed and said not a word. His eyes wandered timidly over all this splendor. Perhaps he did not understand that it was all his.

"Pax tecum," said the sister, thinking that perhaps he understood Latin. And did he!

In one swift movement, as though fearing the good fairy might repent her good deed, he swept up all the toys, stuffed them under his vest, and carried them over to his corner. When his booty had been safely stowed away, he came back on tiptoe, made a respectful bow, and placed a delicate kiss on the nun's hand. From whom could he have learned that? From his father, perhaps?

The sister almost began to believe he had. For when Gino finally woke, he straightway offered to accompany her back to the pilgrims' hospice. Only she had to promise to make a detour round the nearest police station.

And in addition, of course, she had to take the bambina.

Now that the toys had been removed there was ample room for the bambina in the bag. Gino produced another cat-skin, so that his offspring could undertake the march through Rome bedded as softly as possible. And then they stepped out into the dazzling light of day.

Amazed, Palmiro watched them go. Was the good lady coming back soon? For two hours he lived in hopes, then his father returned alone. Palmiro understood. He crept into his corner, pulled out the wax elephant, and pressed it so tightly to his heart that it melted into a sad little lump, hardly bigger than the tears that would not stop trickling down his cheeks.

The sister got back just as the pilgrims were assembling in front of their hospice for their walk to the Lateran. There was a general chorus of rejoicing. The news of her strange disappearance had been quick to spread, and everyone had suddenly realized how much they liked their quiet, unobtrusive companion. The most alarming suppositions had been voiced. Baron von Neuhaus had suspected a plot on the part of the communists or some gang of kidnappers; the schoolmistress had, at her own expense, hired a detective to come at nine o'clock ("Since the gentlemen in charge of the party cannot bestir themselves to make some practical move"); Luitpold the sacristan had not ceased to shake his head, muttering that that was what happened when nuns went gadding about instead of staying in their nunneries; and Eve Süss had got up half an hour earlier in order to go to a nearby church and say a whole rosary for the sister's safe return.

The monsignor did not know whether to hold out his arms or angrily put them behind his back. But seeing that the sister was exhausted to the point of collapse was too much for his good Swabian heart.

"Glory be to God, you are back!" he cried, offering her his arm and leading her inside the house to protect her from a hail of anxious questions. He pushed forward an arm-chair. The sister reeled onto the cushions. But she kept a firm grip on the bag in her hand.

"Before you say anything, you must first get your strength back," decided the monsignor. "Will you have milk or coffee?"

"Both. Coffee for me."

"And milk for whom?"

She opened her bag without a word. The monsignor stood speechless.

When the pilgrims, on their return from the Lateran, heard of Annaberta's adventure in Trastevere, they wanted to give her a jubilant welcome back. Monsignor Schwiefele had to employ all his energy to keep the parish youth group from storming the terrace on the roof, where the sister was catching up on her lost sleep. As a kind of consolation prize he offered them a look at Annaberta junior. Slumbering in a snow-white cot, the cat-catcher's daughter lay absolutely oblivious of all the ladies who, sighing out their comments on this strange event, filed past her one by one.

7. *Concerning the grace none of them had, or why Birnmoser forgot his good intentions*

Because that day was a holyday of obligation, and also the last day in Rome, no definite plans had been made, and the pilgrims could choose for themselves whether they went to the Pontifical Mass in Saint Peter's, or to Saint Paul's, or anywhere else, with the proviso that no pilgrim was to go anywhere without someone who knew the city and its language. The majority turned their steps towards Saint Peter's. The schoolmistress joined up with the chaplain, who intended to show his young protégés the Collegium Germanicum. No student of German language and literature could have approached Goethe's house in Weimar more humbly than did the devoted youth-club members their chaplain's Alma Mater; shyly, talking only in whispers, the young ladies and gentle-men of Kohlenpott trod these sacred halls. The curt greetings of the clerics bustling across the inner courtyard in tomato-red cassocks were returned by the schoolmistress with submissive nods of the head, as though she were anxious to recommend herself as a dutiful child of her diocese to any future bishops. Apart from the windowless church, however, there was little to see in the Germanicum, and so they had plenty of time to go over to the Vatican and swell the crowd of two hundred thousand people awaiting the Pope's blessing to two hundred thousand and twenty.

People of all complexions were pressed cheek by jowl in the wide sweep of Saint Peter's Square, their sunglasses, field-glasses or just their eyes trained on the balcony above the portals of the basilica. As the door to this balcony finally moved, the crowd's nervous muttering was hushed to breathless expectation. It was but the calm before the storm. For as soon as the figure of the Holy Father came into view, a head taller than the prelates standing round him, then the gun-barrels of southern enthusiasm bombarded the balcony with shrieks of "Evviva!," the northerners revved up the engines of their well-meaning oratory, fathers hoisted their handkerchief-waving sons on their shoulders, mothers wiped tears from their eyes—but why should we take the trouble to describe this scene all over again? Every Easter, a whole generation of reporters uses up all its descriptive faculties on this same task. And even so, anyone who has not had the privilege of being present will never be able to know, or even guess, how moved are these two hundred thousand people as they bow down under the blessing of the Holy Father, and how proud they are to be children of the Holy Church.

Sister Annaberta was not kneeling in this joyful throng. But let us hope that the blessing touched her with its wings where she lay in a pleasant half-sleep on the terrace, chatting to the sun and calling the many domes and campaniles by the names of her orphan children. The scarlet fireball still hung in the sky above Trastevere, soon it will wander over the Janiculum towards the Vatican, and at last betake itself to rest behind the Monte Mario. Gino will once more be creeping out after cats, and this time, no stray nun will hinder his murderous handiwork. Oh, Gino!

She suddenly heard Birnmoser's voice: "Well, Sister, are you feeling better?"

"Yes, thank you, Herr Birnmoser. I only wish little Annaberta was as fit as I feel."

"Is something wrong with her?"

"She isn't crying. She lies absolutely quiet in her cot, and just blinks her eyes from time to time. She seems to have very little will to live. I'm so afraid she might die on the journey home."

"But you mustn't let that upset you, Sister. The child is sure to start crying at the right—or should I say the wrong?—moment; when we are trying to get some sleep, in fact. By the way, I should like to invite you to dinner."

"Me? That is impossible, Herr Birnmoser."

"You'll see just how possible it is."

"If you intend to invite me out somewhere, I must refuse."

"To somewhere respectable."

"That makes no difference. What would the monsignor say?"

"But he is coming too. Besides, your mother superior ordered you to obey the monsignor and myself in everything. Twice you have been disobedient. Would you risk a third time?"

A smile escaped Annaberta.

"You certainly know your job," she said. "But surely we are going back this evening?"

"Not until after eleven. We have lots of time before then. Nearly all the pilgrims are going out somewhere beforehand. Chaplain Schlüter is taking his young people to see the fountains at Tivoli. The older generation can't make up its mind between the Via Appia and a beerhouse near the Piazza Colonna."

"But why do you want me to come out with you?"

"To celebrate an engagement," replied Birnmoser, looking very severe.

"Who's getting engaged, then?"

"Eve Süss——"

"And you! Even though you told me a little while ago that you weren't thinking of getting married?"

"When did I say that?" asked Birnmoser in a small voice.

"Three days ago, in the Colosseum."

"Three days ago? My goodness, how quickly a man forgets his good intentions." They both roared with laughter; but Annaberta junior remained silent.

Punctually at six o'clock—Annaberta senior had just given the child a meal of gruel—a taxi drove up. Birnmoser appeared in a sleek black tuxedo, Eve the brimstone yellow had transformed herself into a cabbage white, the monsignor had on a clean collar, and the young priest was immaculately shaven.

They took their seats.

"Trastevere, San Callisto," Birnmoser called to the driver.

"Trastevere?" Annaberta stirred uneasily.

"Don't be afraid. This evening you are safe from cat-catchers."

The lovely evening had enticed all Rome out into the streets. In the crowd on the Corso, Annaberta thought she recognized Simmerl and the sacristan. They were arm in arm, addressing a shoe-shine with feverish sign language, in which the gesture of drinking predominated. "They can hardly be looking for the Via Appia," thought the sister. "So I needn't feel ashamed in front of them."

But she felt all the more ashamed of her pleasure-seeking when they came across the impoverished von Neuhaus couple in the Lungotevere. The baron, hanging like a crumpled umbrella on his wife's arm, dragged himself painfully over the millennial pavements as though he had more blisters than toes on his feet.

Birnmoser ordered the taxi to stop and called out to the pair: "Where are you walking to?"

"To Saint Peter's," replied the baroness.

"But why not take the bus? It stops there."

The baron pricked up his ears. "Did you hear that my dear?" he said. "We could take the bus."

"Be quiet, Ferdinand," she commanded, and he cowered like a whipped spaniel. "We vowed to make a pilgrimage on foot round all the seven basilicas. Having held out till now, we can surely manage the last little bit." And she slapped her husband encouragingly on the back.

"Please, let's drive on," whispered Eve Süss. And neither she, nor Birnmoser, nor the young priest, least of all Annaberta, spoke a word until they drew up in a narrow street of Trastevere.

Sister Annaberta saw little of the gaily decorated restaurant, in front of which even cars from the Vatican were parked. She went through the room with lowered eyes. A long staircase led down to the basement. Only there, where it was delightfully cool and quiet, did she venture to lift her head. And what did she see?

Emerenz Obermair, honored and esteemed spinster (words which one day will be engraved upon her tomb), sat all by herself at a table with a glass of brown liquid in front of her, humming the alto line of Haslbacher's Mass for Saint Cecilia and beating time with the liqueur bottle.

"What the—?" burst from the monsignor, who could scarcely stifle his laughter. "What the—?" echoed the others.

The worthy Emerenz did not notice them until Schwiefele tapped her on the shoulder; then she started out of her blissful ecstasy, dropping the bottle.

Birnmoser inquired how she had managed to find her way here.

Emerenz wiped her damp mouth in shame, violently blew her nose to play for time, and finally launched into an involved explanation. She had decided to gain as many indulgences as possible by visiting every shrine in Rome. She had therefore spent the whole day scurrying like a mouse through catacombs known only to the initiated. Finally she had heard of the well of Saint Callistus, one of the most remarkable shrines in the city. She had hesitated somewhat on finding that this sacred place was situated in a restaurant and bar. But not for long. An amiable waiter had taken her to the well, had described to her most impressively the martyrdom of Pope Callistus, who had been drowned there, and finally had asked if she would like to try some of the water; it was a curative as well as a sanctified drink. Emerenz, with her hunger for relics and her thirst for indulgences, had naturally accepted the offer, and now she was devotedly tasting the revered liquid. And she had to admit that it exceeded by far the waters from any miraculous well that she had hitherto tasted.

"The waiter knew what he was about," said Birnmoser, trying hard to keep a straight face.

"Oh, he is such a god-fearing man. The tears were rolling down his cheeks as he told me how the saint blessed his enemies even as they threw him down the well. I was so grateful, I gave him all the dollars I had left. The poor man has ten children to feed."

Emerenz's eyes glistened with emotion. Then she led the others to a dark alcove, and showed them the well in which the heathens had drowned Pope Callistus.

Sister Annaberta shuddered: "God in heaven, how can I possibly enjoy a meal here?"

"But Sister," the monsignor calmed her, "Saint Callistus has long been enjoying his meal at the marriage feast in heaven. Besides, I am sure the Lord prefers us to sing a 'Te Deum' and drink wine rather than to drink water with a wry face and grumble about the times we live in."

"Quite, Father," remarked Eve. "But He would like it best of all if we sang a 'Te Deum' *and* drank water."

"Naturally," replied the monsignor, "if anyone has so much grace—"

That evening none of them had. They summoned the waiter. He shortly came tripping down the stairs and gallantly served a bottle of Orvieto Bigi. He nodded amicably across to Emerenz, but as he was about to fill Annaberta's glass, he suddenly quivered, spilling a few drops on the tablecloth.

"What's the matter? Don't you feel well?" Birnmoser asked him.

"Niente, signore, niente," he hastily said, quivering all the more. Surprised, the nun raised her head, looked at the waiter, and began to quiver herself.

"What's the matter, Sister? Don't you feel well?" Eve asked.

"Oh, niente, signore, niente," she answered, and on everyone's exploding with laughter to hear her suddenly speak Italian, she regained her self-control, and with a sovereign gesture she motioned to the waiter to fill her glass.

When the waiter had disappeared—rushing up the stairs as if in flight—Birnmoser remarked that he must be a temporary assistant. Birnmoser had never seen him before, even though he knew the place very well.

It was Gino. The sister, however, did not give the game away. Birnmoser would have been sure to call in the police. Then she would have had to put little Annaberta in a children's home. There was, on the other hand, a risk that Gino had meanwhile regretted giving away his daughter and might want her back. Now, each time steps sounded on the stairs, the sister trembled, anxiously peeping to see if it was a policeman coming. But each time it was just Gino, bringing first a dish of cold meat, then more wine, and finally thick cigars. Thus, quite unbeknown to the others at the table, the two of them fought a secret duel, glancing suspiciously at one another while trying desperately to look unconcerned. That Annaberta ate and drank little the monsignor ascribed to the account of the death of Saint

Callistus. He thought that probably the ghost of the drowned pope was haunting away her appetite.

Alois Süss, who had merely picked at the tasty dishes of his ordination dinner and despised earthly pleasures ever since, had regained his old *joie de vivre.* A fuller stomach dispelled his tendency to yawn incessantly. He began to recount pranks played in his student days, imitating famous professors, and made his companions roar with laughter. Eve and the monsignor needed no encouragement to follow suit, one joke led to another, until the pilgrims' spiritual leader, clutching his heaving paunch with one hand, leaned over his glass and said:

"If only the evangelists had reported the jokes our Saviour made at the wedding feast of Cana! They must have been the best in the world."

Every head nodded joyfully, Emerenz alone turning up her nose, as though she were the grandmother of the Inquisition.

Time passed like the wind. The newly ordained priest had let himself be tempted into smoking a cigar—the first he had ever had—and was now growing visibly paler and more silent. At nine o'clock a swarm of American art students flooded the cellar, their noise and their flirting impeded neither by the revered well nor the reverend priesthood present.

"I think we should go. Nobody has forgotten anything?" said the orderly Birnmoser, looking on all the chairs.

"Our engagement, Adam," whispered Eve.

They all stood thunderstruck. But what difference did that make? Once more Gino had to be called, one more glass had to be emptied to the health of the engaged couple. Then they forced a path through the noisy mass of boys and girls, and went up the stairs towards the exit. Gino opened the door. The monsignor and Birnmoser slipped a princely tip into his hand. "Grazie," he said.

As Sister Annaberta passed through the doorway, for the first time that evening they looked straight into each other's eyes. Gino suddenly bent low, impetuously seized the nun's hand, and kissed it, stammering:

"Mille grazie, Suora, mille grazie."

"Well, there's a dashing cavalier for you!" said Birnmoser with a laugh. It was a good thing the sister was standing in shadow, or he would have seen that she was in tears.

The newly ordained priest Alois was feeling unwell, and was impatient to get home. His sister pushed a tablet into his mouth and proposed that they should return via Saint Peter's Square, to see the church floodlit for the feast-day.

No sooner said than done.

And so, a few minutes later, they stood once more in the square that Annaberta loved so much. The fountains were still shooting up towards heaven, their water drops glittering golden in the light of the arc lamps and torches. The church was wearing its cupola like a shining crown. And then it seemed to the sister that this immense structure was growing up and up towards the stars—or were the stars sinking down upon it?—as if the two wings of its colonnade were stretching out like arms to enfold all mankind, everyone in the world, and to lead them home, all those of good will.

"Heaven is—heaven is—" Annaberta said gently. Only Eve heard, for she had offered the tired sister her arm, and now stood next to her.

"Yes, and I think we could go on looking for all eternity, without ever growing tired——"

"As in our own country, as at home."

They said good-bye to Rome as the first lights went out along the façade of the church. Slowly they walked back across the square, silent so as to hear once more the song of the fountains.

Exhausted as she was, Annaberta rushed upstairs to her room as soon as they got back to the hospice, to ask one of the girls from the parish youth group, a housemaid, who had been watching over the child: "Did she cry?"

The girl shook her head:

"No, she still hasn't."

Annaberta was deeply sad. She suspected that Gino had kissed her hand in vain.

8. *Concerning the last battle of love and law, or why they all sang: "We praise Thee, O God"*

With a pilgrimage it is the same as with a story, and with a story it is the same as with a sermon: if it lasts too long, people begin to yawn behind their hands. We will be brief. And let us calmly draw a veil over the fact that when Monsignor Schwiefele checked over his charges, he first counted two too many, then two too few, decided that by the law of averages everyone must be present, and did not realize until Orvieto that in fact Emerenz Obermair, spinster of independent means, was missing. She had left the station to go back to the hospice and collect a case full of consecrated rosaries and candles that she had left behind. The monsignor and Chaplain Schlüter racked their brains wondering what machinery would have to be set in motion before they regained possession of their lost sheep. They decided to use the time between arrival and departure at Florence to institute a full-scale search. But who should be there on the platform, beaming with joy, when they arrived? Emerenz Obermair, none other. She had managed to catch the next connection—though in her youth she had missed many—and the rapido had, according to schedule, brought her to Florence ahead of our pilgrim band.

Monsignor Schwiefele heaved a sigh, and sank immediately into a profound sleep. In the last carriage, the old crowd had once more got together. Eve Süss had moved to the seat next to Annaberta, so as to help her look after Annaberta junior. But the knowledge she had gained from a course in child welfare was as powerless as the nun's many years of experience to explain the little creature's absolute silence, which would have done credit to a Trappist monk. Even the schoolmistress's pedagogical sounding-lead could find no firm ground here.

All in all, the journey home was turning out to be far less gay than the journey there. But then, the pilgrims had no cause for happy anticipation. They knew what awaited them at home. Baroness von Neuhaus was already preparing herself for more bitter feuds with her daily help; Luitpold the sacristan was to be greeted by his old woman, broom in hand; and the newly ordained priest by a directive from his bishop to take up a post as third chaplain in an industrial parish. They were all exhausted into the bargain. Even at Stazione Tibertina, many were already sinking into a leaden sleep, to snore their way right through to the frontier. Chaplain Schlüter, obviously infected with southern nonchalance after all, did not bother to quarter all his protégés in one carriage. And so the equator separating the white sausage of the south from the red sausage of the north, which in the first days of the journey had lain like a secret frontier between the pilgrims, was liquidated. The hop-farmer Simmerl was chatting comfortably with a dozen Rhenish youths and maidens, mentally amazed at their effortless command of the imperfect tense and the subjunctive mood, two aspects of the German language which, like sweetened beer, arouse lifelong antipathy in a staunch Bavarian.

In brotherly concord did the pilgrims thus pray, whisper, snore and gossip their way towards the Brenner Pass. It grew light at Bologna, the sun nodded in through the window at Verona, the monsignor awoke at Trent, and the train stopped for a breather at Botzen. This gave them a chance to stamp their feet and look after their stomachs. Little Annaberta still made no sound.

Just after Brixen, Monsignor Schwiefele stepped into the compartment. Anxiety showed in his face as he looked at the baby.

"What are we going to do at the Customs? We've no export licence for this child."

Yes, of course, none of them had thought of that. The schoolmistress hotly disagreed, declaring that even in Rome she had pointed out how important it was to procure papers for Annaberta junior; but no one apart from herself could remember her having made such a statement. Now the situation was becoming ticklish. The good sister might, in the last resort, be put behind bars for abduction.

"Never!" cried the baron in rage. "We shall defend her to the last drop of our blood!" His eyes blazed, as though he were possessed by the spirits of his ancestors, notorious Bohemian robber knights.

The news of the danger that threatened had already passed from mouth to mouth, and now advice rained down from all quarters. Emerenz Obermair counselled refuge in prayer to Saint Matthew, who was himself a Customs man. Someone else suggested sticking a label on the door of the compartment bearing the word "Diphtheria." Hot-headed Rhinelanders offered to bar the way to the Customs men. But no solemn imperfect, no resounding subjunctive, could be of any help—Annaberta junior had no papers, and whoever has no papers does not exist.

They had already passed Gossensass, best known for a spoonerism. Inexorably the train grunted up towards the Brenner Pass.

"Just push the child under the seat. These Italians don't search very thoroughly, especially a nun's belongings," Eve finally advised, and they all thought that the best idea. The schoolmistress alone declared that she felt painfully *froissée* at thus conspiring to *tricher* the authorities, but as no one apart from herself knew the meaning of *froissée* and *tricher*, her scruples carried no weight.

So Annaberta junior and her basket were consigned to the space under the seat. There was no need, fortunately, to fear any harrying tactics on her part. While the Customs officials were clearing the first carriages, each passenger in the last prayed desperately that the danger would be safely by-passed.

A Customs man entered, cheerfully saluting.

"Good morning. Anything to declare? Wine? Coffee? Cigarettes? Any other unused articles?"

All shook their heads vigorously, too vigorously. Sister Annaberta alone held hers stiff and unmoving.

"And you, Sister? Nothing to declare?"

Every eye was turned on Annaberta, but before she

could open her mouth, Annaberta junior unpityingly laid claim to all attention by emitting a piercing scream. The sister and her fellow conspirators ought actually at that moment to have turned pale with fear, but their joy at the long-awaited cry made them forget all about Customs men, regulations or grave consequences, and clapping their hands they rejoiced: "She's crying! She's crying! Annaberta's crying!," pulled out the basket from under the seat, and crowded round to enjoy a heart-warming view of that open little mouth. There was a stir in the neighboring compartments, and the parish youth club members of both sexes came pouring along the corridor, the boys waving their caps and the girls their scarves:

"She's crying! She's crying!" Tears came into the housemaid's eyes. The monsignor's glasses slid down his nose, and the chaplain's breviary from his hand.

The Customs man was nonplussed for a moment, then he strove to arrange his features into a regulation stiffness, and snapped in broken German: "What is this child? In what passport is entered?"

No one took any notice; all who had a heart to feel were pressed round the basket, where Annaberta junior was screaming so loudly, she might have intended later on in life to become a Wagnerian singer.

The Customs official did not give up the fight.

"That is an Italian child," he said.

Eve turned on him: "Ah, I suppose you can tell that from her accent."

Oh, Eve, Eve, if only you hadn't said that. Now you have made him angry as well as curious.

"Is none of your business, signorina," he wrathfully exclaimed.

"I beg your pardon," retorted Eve cuttingly, planting herself straight as a candle in front of him, "in fact, it is my child."

A deathly silence froze the compartment. The sister's heart was thumping with fear. Eve smiled. The eyes of the Customs official flickered nervously.

"Pardon, pardon signorina, but—but in your passport I read nothing about a child. Where—where was child when you enter Italy?"

"What a silly question. It wasn't here then."

The official looked round helplessly. He encountered nothing but heads nodding in confirmation.

"No, it wasn't here then," seconded the baroness gravely, while the parish youth group struck up a spoken chant so loud that it deafened and blinded the guardian of Customs regulations:

"Hurrah, hurrah, it wasn't here! Hurrah, hurrah, it wasn't here!"

"Then—" the poor man blushed, "may I congratulate, signora, and excuse me please."

When, after a deep bow, he had disappeared, Birnmoser rushed to Eve and pumped her hand up and down:

"Eve, that was marvellous."

The heroine merely smiled.

Annaberta said: "But you need not have hidden the truth for my sake."

"It was the truth. She is my child, or rather she will be, when she is a few years older and Adam and Eve Birnmoser have given her a little playmate. Then we shall come along to your orphanage and collect the cat-catcher's daughter."

Adam and Eve Birnmoser—

"Whew, but that was quick!" the sacristan let out.

"Ferdinand, it took us ten years," the baroness sighed.

"And they say we Bavarians are a slow lot," interpolated Simmerl.

"The pilgrimage is particularly blessed," said the monsignor.

Only Sulamith did not share in the general rejoicing. She pursed her lips and quoted Schiller:

> "Be sure, when you your heart for ever bind,
> That you a heart with true love find,
> For passion's short, and rue is long."

So there we are, and that was the last surprise of the

journey. The farther north they went, the louder did Annaberta junior scream. Late in the afternoon the train steamed into Munich's main station. The two priests—this time in unison—had shortly beforehand sung another "Te Deum" through the loudspeakers, and everyone had joined in with fervor: "We praise thee, O God." Then came the hand-shaking, the promises to write soon, and to make the next pilgrimage together, to Lourdes perhaps, or Fatima, but preferably to Rome once more. Chaplain Schlüter invited the Birnmosers to spend their honeymoon in the Rhine valley, and Simmerl invited the "imperfect" parish youth group to come hop-gathering in the Hallertau. The baroness appointed Monsignor Schwiefele as her spiritual adviser, Emerenz Obermair promised to send the baron her collection of poems, "Roses of Saint Rita."

On seeing the imposing form of Reverend Mother Potentia in the crowd waiting at the station, Sister Annaberta felt a stitch of conscience prick her side, and she began to wonder how the reverend mother would receive the newcomer to the orphanage. But when she overheard the schoolmistress say: "That poor nun! What did she get out of the trip? Nothing but bother with that child," then she felt as rich as a queen, and bending low over her basket she confided her great secret in a whisper to little Annaberta:

"You see, the children of this world aren't always cleverer than the children of light."

And you couldn't have persuaded her that the cat-catcher's little daughter was too young to understand.